BROCABULARY

Also by Daniel Maurer

Six Feet Under, Six Inches In: The Complete Necrophiliac's Guide

BROCABULARY

THE NEW MAN-I-FESTO OF DUDE TALK

DANIEL "DANIMAL" MAURER

ILLUSTRATIONS BY STIRLING SNOW

COLLINS LIVING
An Imprint of HarperCollinsPublishers

HarperCollins books may be purchased for educational, business, or sales promotional use. For information please write: Special Markets Department, HarperCollins Publishers, 10 East 53rd Street, New York, NY 10022.

FIRST EDITION

Designed by Renato Stanisic
Illustrations by Stirling Snow

Library of Congress Cataloging-in-Publication Data

Maurer, Daniel, 1978–
   Brocabulary : a new man-i-festo of dude talk / Daniel "Danimal" Maurer.—1st ed.
      p. cm.
   ISBN 978-0-06-154756-0
   1. Men—Humor. 2. Vocabulary—Humor. I. Title.

PN6231.M45M385 2008
818'.5402—dc22
                                                        2008016136

08 09 10 11 12 ov/RRD 10 9 8 7 6 5 4 3 2 1

DUDE-ICATED to my bro, Pablo,
and my brother from another, Brando

CONTENTS

BROLOGUE

(n.) A prologue that delves into the rich history of bro-speak

According to manthropologists, the first bros were even more primitive than current-day ones—"watching the game" meant looking for animals to kill, and "doing shots" meant throwing spears in the air. Back then life was mostly about meat feasts, and as a result bros spoke in a sort of "arse code" that was comprised of farts and sharts: Three one-cheek sneaks followed by a Hershey squirt meant "Whattup bro?"; a couple of butt burps followed by a triple flutterblast meant "How's it hanging?"

Around 4000 BC a Mesobrotamian started marking in clay every time he got trim. Next thing, he was using symbols to keep track of which chick was which.

Soon Egyptians were using **guy-roglyphics**, a form of writing that was decoded when a couple of bar-cheologists excavated a piece of a bathroom wall from a "titi bar"

(a bar where Nefertiti was worshipped). On it, a Greek dude translated what some Egyptian had written before him, correcting the Egyptian's spelling and calling him a douche. By decoding the Brosetta Stone, linguists discovered that:

actually meant:

Here I Sit, Taking a Shit

During Greek civilization, broing really came into its own. At symposiums, chillosophers would do Jell-O shots while debating timeless topics such as "Who farted?" (Plato's take was "He who smelt it, dealt it"; Aristotle contended that "He who denied it, supplied it.") These bro-downs were often called "sausage parties," since souvlaki was served. Wives and daughters were banned, but so-called "flute girls" were on hand for the oft-requested "skin flute" solo. When their hands were full, dancing girls often applauded a speaker by way of a "booty clap."

The Greeks spent so much time partying down and hitting

the gym that they eventually fell to the Broman Empire, which suffered its own schism when Brutus stabbed his best bro Caesar, prompting his famous last words: "Not cool, dude." This gave rise to the expression "Let's do this like Brutus." Meanwhile over in Jerusalem an alternate phrase was being born.

Jesus, or "Dr. J," was the ultimate bro—he called his dad "Broseph" and demanded his bropostles wear sandals (his stance on backward baseball hats is unknown). Shortly before his death, JC told his dudesciples that he wanted "one last meat hang." He was referring, of course, to sacrificing the Passover lamb and hanging it by its hindquarters, but when the J-Man saw twelve dudes gathered around a table he said, "Christ, this really *is* a meat hang. Anyone know any chicks we can call? You're *killing me*! Or one of you scrotes will, anyway . . ."

Soon after this, the phrase "Let's do this like Judas" became popular, though not as popular as "I'll follow you like Bartholemew," a reference to Jesus's main man that you'd use when tailing your bro to a party. And what did Biblical types say when calling passenger seat? "*Sling*-shot!"

Several hundred years later another cock flock hit the scene. They were the Knights of the Round Poker Table—a royal pussy patrol searching for Holy Tail. Sir "Depants-a-lot" Lancelot never found the coveted pimp cup but he *did* locate the g-spot of King Arthur's wife, breaking the rule of "it shall never be said that a small brother has injured or slain another brother"—which was later simplified to "bros before hos."

During the late eighteenth century, the British colonies got sick of being ruthlessly hazed and were like, "Screw this, let's start a frat of our own!" The Brits laughed it off, thinking the colonists were too nerdy to score any chicks, but everything changed after the Boston Teabagging Party. The "pounding fathers" developed a reputation as master chuggers. A brewery was even named after Sam Adams.

Ben Franklin, whose motto was "it's all about the Benjamin," once got so tanked that he accepted a dare to fly a kite in a lightning storm (keep in mind, this was two hundred and fifty years before *Jackass*). When he was inevitably electrocuted, Thomas "Chocolate Chaser" Jefferson was like, "Oh shit, he's lit!" and the expression has referred to drunken brofos ever since (same with the hangover phrase, "I'm totally fried.") Incidentally, Franklin is known as the inventor of the glass harmonica, but he was much prouder of his *skin* harmonica.

> *"Beer is proof that God loves us and wants us to be happy."*
> —ACTUAL BEN FRANKLIN QUOTE

> *"I cannot tell a lie.* Psych!*"*
> —SOMETHING GEORGE WASHINGTON MAY HAVE SAID

Likewise, George Washington often got loaded to the point of spanking strippers with his powdered wig, something his bros called "wigging out." After he broke his teeth using them as bottle openers, he had to get wooden dentures. He couldn't afford gold fronts because he blew all his money on pole dances—there's a reason he's on the one dollar bill.

There were many bros after that—Mason and Dixon killed a keg and agreed they would piss a line separating North and South. Lewis and Clark went on an even more epic road trip. One night, Lewis told his bro to go make shelter and Clark was like, "Dude, I already *am* pitching a tent." Lewis cracked up and was like, "Holy shit, you could start a campfire with that thing!" The term "skin flint" was born. The two were best of bros till Lewis wrote in his diary that Clark was "cockblocking" him from Sacagawea. It's true they discovered many species of animals, but that word was obviously the best thing to come out of their trip.

During World War II, a regiment known as the "band of bros" invented the expression "jumping on the grenade" when they stormed the bitches of Normandy. But the uber bros of the time were Winston Churchill and Franklin D. Roosevelt, a couple of hard-drinking, cigar-smoking members of the broalition. When Lady Astor once told Churchill he was drunk, he famously responded, "Yes, Madam, and you're ugly. But in the morning, I will be sober and you will still be ugly." Later, during a round of murderball, Churchill confessed to FDR that he kind of wanted to tap that, saying that Lady Astor was a MILF—a "Matriarch I'd Like To Fuck." FDR said, "Really? *But her face!*" To which Churchill responded, "So she's a butterface—like you'd care if you had your beer goggles on." FDR retorted, "Maybe if I brown-bagged it." Churchill didn't miss a beat: "Or *double*-bagged it!" In one fell swoop, several more words were added to the lexicon.

Since then, the dick-tionary has, of course, expanded, but there's evidence that even as bros are celebrated in popular culture (witness the frat pack, as well as the lesser known "sack pack" comprised of Cisco Adler and others), guy-talk has become staler than leftovers from a big-sausage pizza orgy. Chicks eager to "bro along" have started using even the foulest of words, and have taken it upon themselves to invent expressions like "man date." Everyone knows that a "man date" has nothing to do with grabbing a bite with your bro—if anything it refers to the date you became a man by bagging your first stripper. Which raises the question—what's it called when you hook up with a dancer and she leaves *you* the tip?

Despite the best efforts of our manscestors, there are still situations that can't be described using snappy **heologisms**. Which is where this awesome book comes in. By offering up words like **stripper flipper**, *Brocabulary* will expand the male lexicon, fueling **dude-scussions** about everything from sports, to sex, to sex with female sports stars (tennis players, not golfers). What you're holding is more than merely a glossary of **bromenclature**. It's a classic work of **shitterature**—consult it on the can while you've **deuceappeared** from a bad date and it will prevent you from getting dumped when you return from your dump. In fact, assuming dudes study this volume as closely as they do fat pole dancers, or **chunky monkeys**, to make sure they aren't pregnant, this volume will lead to greater personal freedom for mankind, just as the Enlightenment's *Encyclopaedia* did before it. So put down your **liePhone**, you **PDA-hole**, and cancel that **masturdate**. It's time for a lesson in cock talk.

1

BROMMUNICATION

(n.) The art of communicating in a brophisticated manner, with or about your bros

They say that right after God created man, he took a rib from him and made a chick. That's actually a bit of a creation myth—the truth is, after God saw that man was good, he created another man and saw that it was *all good*. For many days these bros lived in a veritable "beer garden of Eden" where they could just pick cans of Schlitz off of trees. One day, though, a chick showed up and asked Adam if he could pick a Jell-O shot off of a certain tree he had been told not to touch—Adam figured, why not, if it'll get this girl wasted. Next thing, God was turning on the lights and telling everyone to go home, party's over, if anyone broke anything their parents will be called.

Before this chick screwed everything up, Adam gave his bro a list of rules written on a bar napkin:

THE TEN BROMMANDMENTS

1. I am your bro. Thou shalt not put hos before me.
2. Thou shalt not take the **dudeonym** or **brewdonym** of thy bro in vain.

3. Thou shalt not make unto my forehead while I am passed out any graven image, or any likeness of a cock and balls.
4. Remember the Sabbath day, to keep it wholly devoted to watching football.
5. Honor my father and my mother: No mother jokes.
6. Thou shalt not kill the keg without first pouring me some.
7. Thou shalt not commit adultery. Adults are lame.
8. Thou shalt not steal my girl.
9. Thou shalt not bear false witness, especially when refereeing a game of beer pong.
10. Thou shalt not covet thy neighbor's wife, unless of course she's a MILF.

Ever since these **bro-nos** were first issued, dudes have been broing down with a religious fervor. Strangely, though, the brocabulary one might use to describe these brotesque situations hasn't kept up with the words we use for guy-girl sitches. Argue with your girlfriend and you've had a "lover's spat," but how do you describe a tiff with your bro? The following words should be of some help when you're living—or just describing—the life brotastic.

abroha – A way to say "hello" and "goodbye" to your bro.

brocaine – Cocaine injested during a circle snort.

Whoever said "hugs not drugs" clearly never did blow with their bros. Get four dudes in a room for some serious **keybauchery** and you'll see so many group hugs it's like an episode of *Golden Guys*, with everyone slapping each other on the back and saying "thank you for being a bro." The downside of this **dudephoria** is that it sometimes causes you to **guybernate**. You stay in someone's apartment watching *Scarface* and having **cokeversations** such as: "Fuck, Kill, Marry: Selma Hayak, Penelope Cruz, and Paz Vega." After cutting line after line with a **gramboni** (a credit card that flattens a gram of coke like a Zamboni smoothing over ice), you become extremely **blowquacious** and you talk about poontang all night instead of chasing it. Next thing you know, it's 6 a.m. and you're wearing a **duststache** and having a **dawnversation** about how you have to go to work in a couple of hours. Wouldn't you rather be doing **body blow**? Of course you would. Nothing beats doing bumps off a chick's lumps Neil Patrick Harris–style.

brocrastination – Killing time with your bros in order to avoid something tedious and soulcrushing your girl has in store for you.

Girls never understand why their boyfriends are always flipping through their **brolodexes** trying to find someone—anyone—other than them to hang out with. *"But you were with them last night,"* they'll whine. Yes, and you'll be with them *every* night as long as your only other option is watching *Friends* reruns with her and her diarrhetic cat.

Ironically, brocrastinating often ends up being as tedious as the thing you're avoiding, especially when your bro starts telling **manecdotes** you've heard one too many times, like the one about hooking up with the PanAm stewardess. *Can't he bang someone on JetBlue already? Any airline that still exists? They don't even call them stewardesses anymore!*

Sooner or later you realize you've reached the night's **dudenoument**—when a bunch of dudes who clearly aren't getting laid are sitting around sipping their last three or four rounds discussing all that was and might have been ("Dude, I can't believe you didn't kick it to that one chick—she was eyeing you like you were dog food").

It's good to have a **post-game bro**, but at this point you're likely to be in a state of mild **cock shock** that suddenly there's no more pussy left in the bar. You check your watch and realize that if you head home now, your girlfriend still might give you a beej. It's the **point of ho return**. But your bros aren't going to let you bounce without applying a heavy amount of **beer pressure**.

Refusing to have just one more is a strict violation of **brotocol**—it's worse than if an old lady asked you to help her across the street and you told her to suck it. The **brocial contract** says you're all there to drink until the bar closes, someone gets arrested, or someone gets violently ill. In fact, a **rendez-dudes** is much like an ill-fated space shuttle launch: There's no bailing out and it doesn't end until chunks are flying everywhere.

At some point, though, you're going to have to return to your **significant bother**. That's when you break out the "shit scale" and weigh the crap you're going to take from your boys for bailing on them against the wet bag of shit that's going to be pimpsmacked across your face if you come home sloshed at 4 a.m. slurring, "I missed wha? I thought your mom's birthday dinner was *tomorrow* night . . ."

The solution here is to get your bros so wasted that come morning, they'll have no recollection of your retreat, or better yet they'll tell you how smart you were to have left. Buy them a couple of rounds of Jäger bombs in quick succession and then pull the ol' Irish exit, **disabeering** into the night without any formalities. Should your boys put you on **brojak** and demand to know your **broordinates**, respond with a **galibi** and tell them you're getting blown by some chick you met in the bathroom line. They'll bust your balls for not introducing her to them— "What is she, a whale? You going **Moby dicking**?"—but hey, at least you're getting some. If your girlfriend lets you in, that is.

bro-D. – To o.d. on a bro: "Oh man, don't invite Reggie. I'm kind of bro-D'ing on him. I've seen him three times this week and am suffering **brolonged exposure**."

bropacetic – Copacetic among bros; the opposite of **fellodrama**.

brostalgia – Nostalgia for something you did with your bro or bros.

When you're in your "whoring twenties," you and your bros probably spend about 75% of your time doing awesome stuff and 25% of the time talking about the awesome stuff you did as a teenager. By the time you're in your dirty thirties, it's maybe 50/50 if you're lucky, and by the time you're in your forties, let's face it, you spend 90% sitting around talking about that time your bro was so wasted he asked a cop for directions to the liquor store.

It's fine to indulge in brostalgia, but it'll fall on deaf ears if you do it with a chick. Just like you could care less about how she and her gay best friend had so much fun at the Madonnathon the other night, you can bet she doesn't want to hear about the time you had to pay off *la poli* when the ho house in Tijuana got raided and your best bro literally got caught with his pants down.

The one exception is wedding speeches. Your bro's life is over as he knows it, so it's only right to deliver a **brobituary**. Will your bro be pissed when, in front of his new father-in-law, you reveal that back when he ran the "Whore Club for Men" his business card read "I'm not just the pimp, I'm also a client"? Sure he will be, but that story is a classic that deserves to be shared with everyone.

In fact, why not pass around **brotographs** of the groom. Share those **brodak moments**: "This is him posing with a Ronald McDonald statue after we replaced the head with a severed pig's . . . And here's another one . . . We dared him five bucks to do that to the eye socket . . ."

cerebro – The bro who does the thinking for you. You're R2-D-Dude and he's C-3P-Bro.

Hard partying tends to turn your brain to whiskey mash, so it's croosh to keep a **brofessor** around who can still do things like add and subtract. Sometimes you're such a horndog that you want to give the waitress a 75% gratuity—a move known as **rovertipping**. You might also need him to spell, since it'd be embarrassing if you botched the word "cunnilingus" in the note you're leaving with the tip. And chances are you'll also need him to remember your address when he's putting your vomit-covered ass into a cab. Sure, your BlackBerry can do a lot of this stuff, but can your BlackBerry also make you look good by showing chicks that, yes, smart people do hang out with you?

Having a cerebro as your wingman is pretty choice. When he's talking to a girl, you can pretty much nod and say "totally" at all the incisive stuff he says about the situation in the Middle East or the latest art exhibit or whatever and the girl will assume you know what the hell he's talking about. When your bro disappears, tell her you're tired of all the serious convo—"Can we just forget, for once, the question of liberal or conservative? How about: My place or yours?"

dudeonym – A name that only your dudes call you.

If there's one thing that's croosh to your **dude-velopement**, it's a good nickname—who knows how many Kevins or Bobs or Randys got a second lease on life when their bros rechristened them Hoss or Big Unit. Even our most hallowed Presidents understand the importance of giving their cabinet members uplifting names like Turd Blossom and Scooter. The thing is, you can't choose your own dudeonym. People aren't going to start calling you Teddy Brosevelt just because you start saying, "Talk softly and carry a big dick." Unless of course, you pay one of your bros to do so and hope that it catches on.

dudescussion – A dudes-only discussion.

When you and your bros engage in a dudescussion, brotocol dictates that you be completely **dickscrete**. Sure, you'll be tempted to tell your girl, "You know what Rob said the other day? That he likes to hang out at the pizza stand at 2 a.m. picking up drunken high school girls. I can't believe a 35-year-old guy would stoop to that." Committing **blabotage** is tempting for several reasons: It shows your girl that compared to your bro's, your own boorishness is a walk in the park—granted, a very sketchy park with lots of used condoms and dime bags lying around—and that she should therefore cut you a break next time you come home with the "scent of a stripper" on you; it shows her that you have enough integrity to condemn piggish behavior even when committed by your best buds; and it makes you come off as an honest dude who would tell her anything.

But don't be surprised when your back-stabbing backfires and she tells you she doesn't want you hanging out with Rob anymore, or she starts holding it against you that your friends are reprobates, undermining your every attempt to gain the upper hand with statements like, "What would you know? Your best friend hits on sixteen-year-olds at a pizza parlor."

fellabrate – To celebrate with the fellas: "Jim just got divorced! Fellabration!"

fellodrama – Melodrama between fellows.

Ah, **dudetopia**: No cat fights, no trifling, no pettiness—just rednecks, white socks, and cheap beer, like the song goes. Except that sometimes guys start acting like snitty little bitches, no better than middle-school girls. Of course, there are always **mentanglements** when you're jockeying for posish and attempting to establish yourself as the "leader of the sacks," but fellodrama is something completely different from asserting your god-given right to bang your bro's sister—it's a form of behavior that's completely **assive-aggressive**.

Fellodrama might creep up, for instance, when your bro Jim gets irritated that instead of hanging with him at McCarthy's you met up with your bro John at McCaffrey's. Instead of sacking up and confronting you about it, he tells your other bros that you're **persona non frata**—banned from the frat. He starts **nadmouthing** you, ostensibly sticking his balls in your mouth and "tainting" your reputation. You'll be tempted to go *hermano-a-mano* by bitchslapping him, but this is counter-broductive. These temporary **broing pains** will pass if you skip the throwdown and engage in a **bro-down**—a **two-beer peace summit** in which you attempt to resolve your differences over a couple of brewskies.

fembrace – A feminine embrace that causes you to wonder if a bro is "being straight with you."

When hugging another man (say, when your softball team wins), make sure it starts with a firm manshake, then basically rip his arm off as you bring him to you. You should feel his warm arm-socket blood spraying your face. Slam your fist or open palm on his back hard enough to knock his teeth out. Anything less is a **fembrace**, and will cause him to wonder if it's the pink team you're actually playing for.

frataclysm – Something earth-shattering that befalls a frat: a **fratastrophic** disaster that might lead to the downfall of a Greek empire, as seen in *Animal House*, *Revenge of the Nerds*, *Assault of the Party Nerds*, and *Old School*.

friendjamins – Hundred dollar bills, lent to a friend.

Lending money to a bro is Bad Idea Jeans. Chances are the bro who owes you that $5,000 considers it sufficient payback that he hangs out with you, picks up the occasional Baconator, and tells you about all the trim he gets. In his mind, you're living **guycariously** through his awesome life, and you can't put a price on that. He doesn't seem to realize that the C-note he blew at the casino last night should've gone toward your knee surgery, since you don't have health care. You begin to realize that you'll probably see the U.S. soccer team win a World Cup before you see your money again. To avoid **fellodrama** about this, don't expect your friend-jamins back in the first place—just tell him to get you back in whatever **paltruistic** way he can, for instance by hooking you up with one of his chick friends. Sometimes payback can literally be a bitch.

galibi – An alibi you give your bros to make it look like you bailed for tail.

Ditching a bro for a ho is bad, but it's even worse when you flake because you got sucked into a *Murder She Wrote* marathon. When this happens, you need to save face by concocting a **bail tale** that involves *getting* tail: "Sorry, dude—I was on my way to the bar when my hot neighbor asked me to kill a garden snake. Next thing I knew she was pulling out my trouser snake."

Stories about how you had to "ditch for a bitch" should be vague and impossible to verify. If your bro finds out you lied about getting a BJ, your credibility will be the only thing blown. A galibi will also backfire if it involves romance or chivalry of any kind: *Don't* tell your bros you had to get a girl flowers. *Do* tell them you had to deflower her.

guyamese twins – Two guys who are pretty much inseparable.

Some dudes are so tight that they're practically attached to each other via a **chumbilical cord**. They're like Chang and Eng, or Dumb and Dumber. They have separate brains but they share a liver, drinking together day in and day out. Sometimes one of them will even bang a girl while the other one watches.

A serious **helationship** usually starts with "courtship"—when a guy tries to curry favor with you by telling you he can get you courtside seats to a game. Front-row tickets say, "This is the start of a dude-iful thing."

After you've gone from courtship to full-scale **bromance**, it's only right to **bropose**—ask him to be your lifelong bro. This request usually isn't made outright, but rather in the guise of a different question—for instance, "Will you, John, take me, Tim, to the Super Bowl?" Soon, you'll have him on **heavy brotation**.

Navigating a helationship is tricky, and you're going to encounter **bropponents**—bro bashers who are opposed to your **bromosexual** relationship. Your girlfriend won't understand why you'd rather hang with your dude than bang in the nude. Be careful you don't "bro too far" and cause people to think of you as an "ambiguously gay duo."

GUYAMESE TWINS WHO "BROED THE LINE":

Abraham Lincoln and Joshua Speed: At the age of 28, Honest Abe was hard up for cash and, some say, hard up for a general store owner who shared a bed with him.

Jose Canseco and Mark McGwire: These "ballers" were inseparable back in the late 80s, when they were dubbed the Bash Brothers. Always seen wearing tights and slapping each other's asses, these homo . . . er . . . homer hitters even went so far as to "juice" each other.

Batman and Robin: A 1950s book, *Seduction of the Innocent*, put it this way—"They live in sumptuous quarters, with beautiful flowers in large vases, and have a butler. It is like a wish dream of two homosexuals living together."

Matt Damon and Ben Affleck: At one point these bromos were so inseparable that when Ben asked for a boys' night out, J-Lo told him he should go ahead and marry Matt. Have they done some "good dill hunting" in their time?

Michael Knight and KITT—A wrist communicator, sort of like a wedding band, kept them in touch at all times.

guynamic – The dynamic between bros. "Dude, this Yoko is totally throwing off the guynamic."

ho-blivion – The oblivion that bros sometimes vanish into when they get a ho.

It's fine to put "nudes before dudes" or "trim before him" now and then, but some bros get some and then immediately allow a girl to carry them around in her kangaroo pouch, never to walk like a man again. Their brains are washed in Massengill and they receive a full **brobotomy**. Sometimes they even come right out and ask for a **dudevorce** by taking back the video game system they were keeping at your house.

The behaviors of someone who has disappeared into **ho-blivion** are similar to those of someone who has joined a cult—he begins using new language and jargon ("Sorry I 'can't make it,' but I promised my 'girlfriend' I'd 'lend a hand' with something that 'means a lot to her'"), he distances himself from those not affiliated from the cult, he changes his diet and sleep patterns (no more T-bones since his girlfriend is vegan, no more chasing tail till 4 a.m.), he exhibits humorlessness (especially when you ask him if he got down on one knee when he offered up his balls), and he abandons the three-dimensional threesomes site you were going to launch together, 3D3Sums.com.

Here are some other signs that a man needs to be **dehogrammed**:

pickedout-fits: Outfits that his wife clearly picked out for him. The first thing a woman does to keep her husband from getting **extramari-tail** is to turn his **scoredrobe** into a **boredrobe**. If he's wearing a Gap turtleneck sweater, it's obviously to hide the whip marks on his back.

"we"bonics: The language of coupledom. Every time your bro starts a sentence with "We" or "My wife and I," just say, "Stop right there," and walk away.

co-pinions: When you ask him what he thought of something— say, a movie—and he pulls a "Siskel and Shebert" by responding with something like, "I didn't think it was that funny but Julie *loved* it. I guess it was pretty hilarious."

herfews: A curfew his wife has imposed, usually for **clitiotic** reasons. "Sorry guys, I can't stay past the fifth inning because I have to go wash the dishes left over from my wife's book club . . ."

homieopathy – Hanging with your homies in order to take the hurt off of something like a bad breakup.

hommitment – A commitment you made with a ho that prevents you from hanging out with your bros: "Sorry man, I can't make it to Chugly's tonight, I've got a hommitment. She wants me to go to the hospital to bond with my newborn son. Lame, I know . . ."

Once something is on your **palendar**, it's etched in bone—no ifs, ands, or "but my wife's water broke." It could be twelve hours before the kid pops out—that's plenty of time to honor your **brommitment** to play *Call of Duty*. Often, however, these obligations become **prob-ligations**. On an average Sunday a palendar and a **vagenda**—your girlfriend's agenda—can be very different things. Just remember, you have to have **guyorities**, and it can't be said enough: Bros before hos.

manalyze – To analyze someone you've just met in order to determine his degree of manliness.

When you're introduced to a guy, ask yourself this: Where does he stand on the imaginary masculinity scale? Is he on the far left side holding pink pom poms or on the far right side squeezing a pink bra full of double-D tatas? Within five minutes of convo, you should know the answers to these simple questions:

1. **Does he have a manshake?** When you shake his hand, does it feel like he's trying to crush your fingers into a fine powder so he can snort them off your girlfriend's ass (good) or does it feel like he's forgetting to grip because he's distracted by your beautiful eyes (bad)?

2. **Is he a brofessional?** When you ask him "What do you do?" does he tell you he's a stock car racer or a Blackwater mercenary, or is he a publicist or "personal assistant"?

3. **Is he fandiloquent?** When you ask what he thought of the game last night, does he say he couldn't believe they decided to run on fourth and twelve, or does he say, "*The Game?* Is that a new reality show?"

4. **Does he drink palcohol?** When you ask him what he's having, does he ask for a Bud, or does he give you a fruity drink order like a cosmotini? Or a *really* fruity drink order like "I'll have what you're having [wink]"?

5. **What is his degree of trekspertise?** When you talk about the route that you took to get to the party, does he offer an alternate super-secret route and give you sound advice on avoiding traffic?

6. **Is he carticulate?** When you ask him what he's driving, does he turn into Guysaac Newton, able to explain torque and

horsepower? Does he try to **rimpress** you by telling you what kind of rims he has and saying, "I threw some Ds on that bitch"? Or does he just shrug and say, "I dunno, my girlfriend drove me . . ."

Remember that when you're manalyzing someone, he's doing the same to you. Show him that you're worthy of **palidation**—the sort of validation that will make you good pals—but remember that it's still too early in the game to try to impress him with **bragablowccio** about the last beej you got.

PAL 2000 – when a bro who seems to have your best interest at heart suddenly turns on you like HAL 2000 in *2001: A Space Odyssey*, usually by giving you bad advice and claiming it's for your own good: "The dude was my **brother half** until he PAL 2000ed me by convincing me to dump my girl and then hooking up with her. He totally soaked me in **traitorade**."

paltruism – Selflessly being there for your bro like you're a real Brother Theresa.

sack pack – A bunch of dudes traveling in a group, or a **cock flock**. When they turn into a **door jam** by jockeying to get into a club, they're known as a **bluster cluster**, and when they storm a party they're known as a **bro storm**.

spawnversation – An awkward conversation about your bro's kid.
    In most cases a bro has long vanished into ho-blivion by the time he has a kid. Some bros, however, insist on being **dadolescents**, clueless to the fact that rock and rollers don't push strollers. This guy dresses his kid in **doucheshirts** that say "BOOB MAN" and pisses everyone off by wheeling his yappy youngster into the bar. When a chick does this, there's at least the possibility of some sweet breastfeeding action. But with dudes, it's just a buzzkill, since you have to play the clean version of the "f*** you like an animal" song on the mp3 jukebox.

At this point there's no way to avoid conversations about your bro's kid. You probably won't remember the child's name, sex, or general age, but you can avoid embarrassment by using casual substitutions like "the little munchkin" or "that thing your wife popped out." You'll be tempted to shun the kid for destroying your bro's life as you knew it, but why not use the tot to your advantage? Take him for a walk and use him as babe bait. When chicks approach you and ask, "Who's the mommy?" you can tell them, "Nevermind that. Who's your daddy?"

testosterzone – Places where men gather to be with other men.

In life there are **breastinations** (places where women gather to be with their own) and **testosterzones**. If you're a dude, you definitely don't want to end up at a breastination—unless you're a **Lilith Fairy**, the type of guy who feebly tries to impress chicks by going to lesbian folk singer concerts. No, you're much better off at a **dudist colony** like Rincon, Puerto Rico, where you'll be surrounded by nothing but surf boards, a rich history of waves, and dudes going, "Duuuude!" Here's a handy chart to help you understand the difference.

BREASTINATION	TESTOSTERZONE
There's a mat on the floor so you can do yoga	There's a mat on the floor for when you fly off the mechanical bull
There's tea	There's T&A
You come to rap about your personal feelings	You come to feel up persons while listening to rap
There's Tupperware	There's rubbers
While you stretch for seven minutes, you're repeating a mantra in your head	During the seventh inning stretch, you're beating a man in the head
You're talking about what you thought about the book	You're being booked

BREASTINATION	TESTOSTERZONE
You're surrounded by people in leotards	You're surrounded by retards
You and your friends are getting your nails painted	You and your friends are nailing each other with paint guns
You're telling your friend how cute she'd look in that dress	You're telling your friend how cute the shot girl would look undressed
You're showing off the new ring on your finger	You're giving the finger to someone in the ring
You're in the garden, drinking iced tea	You're at the Garden, watching ice hockey
You're in the yard eating salad and talking about your weight	You're in the yard lifting weights so you won't get your salad tossed

A testosterzone can also refer to a state of heightened primal masculinity. Any number of things can put you there. Sports, for one—witness soccer hooliganism. Or porn—jet fighters have been known to watch it before flying the friendly skies and annihilating the enemy. So the next time *you* need to sack up, try watching porn or sports first. Say you're nervous about asking your boss for a promotion: Take in five minutes of *Sperminator 2* before you march into his office. Just make sure he doesn't catch you or you might be called in to tender your resignation.

Vincent Van Bro – A bro who is so loyal he would cut his ear off for you.

wannabro – A dork who tries to be a bro but is nothing but a wannabe. Sometimes referred to as a **wannaDB**, as in "Dude you're not even a douchebag, you're a **wannaDB**."

2

BARTICULATION

(n.) Articulation that occurs at a bar, or that applies to boozing it and losing it

It's no secret that the French philosophers pounded the ol' vino before coming up with truisms like "I drink therefore I am." In fact, this entire book was written with plenty of gin and juice on hand (nothing wrong with a little bit of **ginspiration**) and it's not the only great work of **obliterature** that was penned between belches. Even the greats like Hemingway and Fitzgerald divided their time between pounding away at their Smith Coronas and just plain pounding Coronas.

A recent study explored the reasons that alcohol makes you smarter and more physically adept: "Research revealed that subjects who drank displayed highly elevated oral capacities. In fact their oral capacities were *almost as awesome as your mom's*!" That study was conducted by a bunch of dudes wearing togas and telling their subjects to "Chug! Chug! Chug!" so its findings—including the fact that hiccups give you more time to think—have been largely discredited. More than likely, its subjects were generating **bartificial intelligence**—the fake intelligence that occurs when you're drunkenly rambling at the bar.

That said, it's pretty much common sense that booze causes people to come out of their proverbial peanut shells. A few Heineys will turn even the most quiet, melancholy soul into a regular **Abraham Drinkin'**, to the point where he'll loosen up and launch into a speech—"Four whores and seven beers ago . . ." In fact the *real* Abraham Lincoln's so-called Emancipation Proclamation was more of an **Inebriation Proclamation**, as evidenced by this letter he sent everyone the next day:

Yo bros,
Obviously I was totally shitcabinned last night. The way I
barely remember it, I turned into Drinkin' Lincoln as usual
(someone should've cut me off when I started talking
about my "Lincoln log"). Clearly I took things too far with
that stuff about freeing slaves. Suffice it to say, the next

round's on me, and by God if it won't be delivered by my own personal servant!

Yours,

A-Rock

The problem with barticulation is that you later disavow or don't remember what it is you slurred in the first place. But there are exceptions. The first time George H. W. Bush referred to "a thousand points of light," he was yelling at one of his bros to close the shades because he had the mother of all hangovers. The whole frat house razzed him for being such a pussy, but the last laugh was on them when he went on to use the phrase in a stirring inauguration speech.

This chapter will provide you with an arsenal of words to use both while you're having a **fargone-versation** and while you're fully sober, whether you're reflecting on whatever horrible, life-shattering mistakes you made the night before or you're planning to make them all over again tonight.

alcofall – A common type of **bingeury** that occurs due to excessive alcohol, also known as a "beer spill."

Swilling booze tends to endow you with Mitch Gaylord–like gymnastic abilities, but sometimes the keg stand goes horribly awry and you suffer an alcofall. It happens to the steadiest of drinkers—even to Keith Richards that time he climbed a tree and foraged for **broconuts** to drink out of with Mick Jagger.

Alcofalls happened a ton back in the days of pirates—think how hard it would be to swig rum and keep yourself balanced on a peg leg while getting blown by a mermaid (mermaids, by the way, are what started that whole "smells like fish" thing). Plus a lot of times one of the pirates would be like, "Watch me walk the plank!" and before anyone could even place bets, he was shark bait.

Many a man's last words have been "yo, check this out," but full-on **alcofallics** are usually chicks who strap themselves into their Manolo Blahnik stilettos and hit the cobblestones of club row knowing full well that after two shots of Cuervo they're going down like a piñata. When this happens you can only point and laugh while you look up their skirts trying to catch a glimpse.

If you're with a victim of an alcofall or suffer one yourself, hit the **barmacy** and fill a prescription for more sweet, pain-killing booze stat. Sometimes the best cure is mouth-to-mouth-of-the-bottle resuscitation. Just make sure your constant drinking doesn't cause you to suffer an alcofall from grace—losing a job, a wife, or your left nut due to Bukowski-esque boozing.

barchipelago – A group of bars clustered together for easy hopping.

barjack – To take over a bar by force, whether by **brolling deep** or by being obnoxious jackasses: "Dude, let's go to Futtbuckers!" "But it's trivia night." "So what, we'll just barjack the place. Put on your boots, there's going to be a bro storm!"

barnacle – Chumps who attach themselves to the bar like barnacles, preventing you from getting a drink.

Sometimes there's a veritable defensive line blocking you from the bartender, except instead of safeties and linebackers you're dealing with a **dorkestra** of first daters debating whether Elijah Wood was right for the part of Frodo. You begin suffering from **peanuts envy** because they're blocking your access to the bar food. Obviously you can't bash their heads together like the Terminator did when he entered the bar (most confusing aspect of that scene: He demands the guy's clothes, his boots, and his motorcycle—*but not his beer?*). However, the following approaches might help drink meet palm faster:

1. **Bailitosis:** Punish the barblockers with your wino-like booze breath and the occasional Barney belch until they can't take it anymore and they bail.

2. **Beerfriend them:** Befriend them by complimenting their beer choice and then ask them if they wouldn't mind ordering you one.

3. **Swaycate the area:** Sway drunkenly into their personal space until they vacate their stools.

4. **Be a flexhibitionist:** Show your barkeep that you're "here for beer" by planting a hand or elbow on the bar. Flex as if to tell the barnacle next to you, "If you even think about complaining about my arm being here, I'll smash that Corona over your head and spritz the wound with a lime."

When a bar is completely covered in barnacles, don't stand in front of the **Mexican drawbridge**—the section that the barbacks lift up and down. You don't want to get in the way of these guys when they're ducking in and out—they're avid soccer players and they won't hesitate to headbutt your balls. Instead try your luck at the waitress station—the waitress will give you **twattitude** for blocking it, but you can always try to **strongcharm** her. Offer to give her your digits if she gets the barkeep's attention and you might just score booze *and* cooze.

bar par – The number of drinks that it's appropriate to consume at a given bar. "Dude, this is the Swiggin' Brigand—you're six shots and one funnel under the bar par."

barsenal – Your alcoholic arsenal. "I always keep absinthe in my barsenal—the stuff is **ginamite**."

barticipate – To participate in something that happens in a bar, or in going to a bar. "We're headed to Babes on Board for a boobs cruise. Barticipation is mandatory!"

barticulars – The details about which bar you're meeting up at, etc.

benderdome – A one-on-one drinking session cum competition between you and your bro in which "two men enter, one man leaves," in the tradition of *Mad Max Beyond Thunderdome*. It's up to you whether you want to go as far as incorporating a Wheel of Fortune that outlines fates such as Amputation, Gulag, or Thirty Hours of Lifetime Television.

bingeury – An injury that occurs during a binge.

Alcofalls aren't the only injuries that will cause you to have a "binge of regret." Thought losing your credit card was bad? Many a man has lost a limb and worse while tying one on, starting with these historical figures:

Franklin D. Roosevelt: For political reasons he pleaded polio, but he was actually confined to a wheelchair after he and his buddies tipped the wrong cow.

Professor Stephen Hawking: This brainy binger was robbed of his faculties while popping wheelies in the Costa Rican sand dunes. Luckily the two hookers who were riding bitch emerged unscathed.

Ludwig Van Beethoven: After passing out, this pint-pounding pianist tragically went deaf when one of his pals thought it would be funny to wake him up with an air horn.

Genghis Khan: One theory about this warrior's cause of death is that an enemy princess pulled a Lorena Bobbitt on him (no joke). But why did he have his precious pecker exposed? Chances are he suffered a **jackout** while engaging in **smashedurbation**.

> Guyku #1
> *Maker's and The Beast*
> *Drank too much of each, Bonzo's*
> *Fate is within reach*
> —Jud Laghi

blottomobile – A car whose passengers are totally blotto.

Nothing beats driving a car that's "fully loaded." Your passengers mix themselves some **cargaritas** and your Geo Prism becomes a "bar car." Then someone busts out the **carcotics** and "makes tracks" on the dashboard—you've got your "snow tires" on! You're doing "speed bumps"! Next thing you know, you've merged onto I-420 and the **rastacarian** in the backseat turns

your vehicle into a "green machine" by starting a "car fire." Someone passes around some E and twenty minutes later you're "rolling down the highway." The guy who's riding shotgun opens the "love compartment" (the glove compartment where you keep your condoms) and starts "burning rubber" with some chick you picked up on the side of the road. Congratulations—you've got yourself a bang bus. A real shaggin' wagon.

Ideally, the driver in these situations is sober as the day he was born (assuming he wasn't born with fetal alcohol syndrome), but everyone has encountered a **breathaliar**—a dude who claims he's all right to drive even though if he got breathalyzered he'd blow higher than his own IQ (which isn't saying much). There's no talking someone like this out of getting his swerve on—he'll just ignore you and probably even **roadkill** a bottle or two on his way home, then grab a six pack from the backseat and commit **voluntary canslaughter**.

If your bro is hellbent on **cansportation** (transporting open beer cans), remind him of a few simple rules from the drunk driver's manual and there's a chance he won't go from taking a shot in his beer mug to getting his mugshot taken:

1. Don't drink and drive.
2. If you do drink and drive, don't drink and drive on the wrong side of the road.
3. Don't drink and drive with your lights off. Same with your pants.
4. Don't drink and drive with your eyes closed. Do keep your doors closed.
5. Don't drink and drive into stuff.
6. Avoid a **rackcident** or a **crackcident:** Don't drink and drive while ogling tits and ass.
7. Don't get into a **jackcident**, either. Like the Doors said in "Roadhouse Blues," keep your eyes on the road and your hands upon the wheel.
8. Don't blow chunks on your windshield. Cars with green-tinted windows are way more likely to get pulled over.
9. Don't hit the DUI-ve thru. Go for a Baconator at Wendy's and you're likely to get baconated by the cops when they see you smash into the "order here" speaker.
10. Should you get baconated, don't take the opportunity to bust out some favorite lines like, "What seems to be the officer problem?" Keep insisting that there's an officer problem and you'll also get to say, "Don't tase me, bro!"

Next time you're pounding bourbon in your Suburban, or having a little pick-me-up in your pickup truck, or getting bent in your Benz, these rules should help keep you on track. And that's on *track*, not on tracks. Railroad tracks are bumpy and driving on them might cause you to spill everyone's **cartinis**.

bombaraderie – A special brand of camaraderie brought on by Irish Car Bombs.

bongversation – A conversation that occurs while a bong is being passed around. These **marijuanversations** usually explore matters of **bongtology**—life as interpreted by people hitting the water pipe.

break fluid – Water, when consumed in order to take a break from drinking or to put the brakes on a drunken mistake. "Good thing I got some break fluid in me or I would've made a move on Bill's fiancée."

brewdonym – Your drinking name.

From the Babe to Fonzy to McLovin, every self-respecting man has a dudeonym—the name under which he accomplishes his proudest **machievements**. But a dudeonym isn't enough—when you're chugging and bugging, you're going to need a **brewdonym**—a name that indicates you're prone to entirely different **beerhavior** when you're tanked. Feel free to steal one of the following:

BREWDONYM	BEERHAVIOR
Abraham Drinkin'	Abandons his usual reticence and becomes extremely barticulate.
Liquardo Montelban	Turns into a Latin playboy, seducing women with his knowledge of Spanish. Also goes by the name Dickhardo Montelban.
Saddam Brewssein	Becomes a tyrant, crushing skulls and killing cheese curds.
Miguel de Swervantes	Swerves excessively while walking or driving, as if impersonating Don Quixote tilting at windmills.
Robert De Beero	Becomes paranoid and repeatedly demands, "You lookin' at me? You lookin at me, punk?"

BREWDONYM	BEERHAVIOR
Doogie Houser	Is underage but houses beers like he's 21.
Harry S. Brewman	Drops sake bombs into his beer. Not a very difficult decision.
Swill Clinton	Affects a Southern accent and talks fat chicks into blowing him in the bathroom.
MC Hammered	Turns into a wannabe gangsta.
Cool Hand Puke	Barfs as if he's just eaten fifty eggs but is totally cool about it.

brew manchu – A Fu Manchu–style mustache created by beer foam.

brewnanimous decision – A unanimous decision made by members of your drinking party as to where to go next, usually a strip club.

brewthanasia – The killing of a beer; also called a **beer death experience**.

brojectile vomit – When your bro gets caught in your chunder-storm.

brorangutan – The apelike creature you become after pounding a few with your bros.

If you were Charles Barwin and you charted the evolution of man over the course of a drinking sesh you would see him progress from being an upright **bromo sapiens** to gradually slumping over as he "puts some hair on his chest" with Cuervo shots, to finally passing out in his own primordial booze somewhere on the way home. That's why if you walk into a bar shortly before last call, you'll see something that resembles the opening sequence of *2001: A Space Odyssey*, except instead of orchestra music playing while apes smash bones on the ground, Journey is playing while hairy dudes slam pints down on the table.

If your boy starts pounding his chest like a **brorilla** or demonstrates any of the following **beerratic beerhavior**, fill him with break fluid fast.

1. **He starts "hulking out."** His skin turns a disturbing color of green, like the Incredible Hulk's, and he grimaces and grunts like a **genetic brewtant**.
2. **He becomes ginsistant.** He yells "Listen to me!" and yet when the table falls silent he just drools.
3. **He has highlids.** His eyelids droop as if he's high.
4. **He launches into a gone-ologue**—a monologue of incoherent mumbling. At this point he's **mutterly wasted**.
5. **He starts foolulating**—loudly ululating like a drunken fool. **Douchecibel** levels elevate.
6. **He saliviolates you.** A sure sign that your buddy has completely turned into a brorangutan is when he tongue rapes your face.

7. **He doesn't grip to sip.** He can't even lift a pint to his lips, and instead stoops over to sip from his beer like a kitten lapping up milk.
8. **He becomes Furious George.** He starts insanely swinging from things, climbing on things, and jumping on things to the point where you have to tell him, "Watch out for that tree!"
9. **He begins throwing his own feces at the walls.** Oh shit!

Once such behavior is observed, there is no stopping your bro from turning into a raving **broboon**. Trying to cut him off or suggesting that he tuck his penis back in before the waitress returns will only loose the primordial savage. Though he might become violently confrontational if he has enough **assholine** in his tank, more often a brorangutan will injure only himself and whatever objects he happens to dive into, fall onto while disrobing, or smash into his own face while doing his best *Elephant Man*: "*I am not an animal!*" Keep a brorangutan away from trash cans and punch bowls, since he is liable to empty them on himself while screaming "Who's the man!" On the other hand, if he asks you if you think he can roof one of his possessions, let him do it—you'll get a good laugh when he senselessly tries to throw one of his shoes onto the roof of a building only to hurl it through someone's window. Above all, keep your **brotal recall** good and attuned since, come morning, he's going to need you to explain why his girlfriend left him again.

brotal recall – A bro's total recall for what you did last night while hit-shammered.

When you wake up with a nasty headache and chunks on your cheeks, you're likely to recall the events of the previous night in the form of a **gonetage**—a montage of just a few select scenes from before you became too far gone to remember anything. You have no earthly idea how you got home or why the words "MANSON LIVES" are crudely tattooed on your forehead. Luckily you can always count on your bro to fill you in, right after he asks fifty times, "Dude, you *really* don't remember what you did last night?"

Brotal recall can be a good thing when you need to know which titty bar you left your credit card at, but it can be bad when you're brunching with your girl and your bro is like, "Dude, you were **transvestanked** the other night—you were *this* close to playing the Crying Game with this chick who had a Madam's Apple."

cock-a-doodle brew – A beer that's consumed first thing in the morning.

fargone-versation – An exchange that occurs while you and the other party are totally far gone.

When world leaders meet, there's always a pitcher of water on hand, which is probably why they never say much beyond, "This is a promising development for peace in the Middle East." We all know that if they were drinking from a pitcher of Abita Purple Haze, the Israeli prime minister would probably end up talking

smack with the Arab sheikh and asking him if he might be willing to throw him a few hos from his harem.

Fargone-versations usually involve a lot of **tequilaborating**—elaborating more than is necessary because your cognitive faculties have been "shot to hell" by tequila. Here's an example:

GUY #1: Dude, you're the best.

GUY #2: Thanks man, that's cool.

GUY #1: I love you, dude. You know you're the only black friend I have?

GUY #2: Thanks. I'm honored, bro.

GUY #1: No seriously, dude. Before I met you I thought black people did nothing but loot and play basketball. Seriously. I love you, man.

GUY #2: Uh . . . okay, man. Maybe we should get you some water?

GUY #1: No dude, you my boy! You my—

EAVESDROPPER: Oh shit, that dude is **MC Hammered**.

As one might imagine, exchanges like the above very easily turn into **barguments**. You're having a fargone-versation with your bro when all of the sudden he goes from boozing it to losing it. It's one thing when someone gets a little **beeritated**, but it's another thing entirely when they become **bingefuriated**.

Before a bargument gets out of hand and turns into an outright **neanderbrawl**, remember what Dalton said in *Road House*: "Nobody ever wins a fight." If that doesn't work for you, remember his other piece of advice: "Shatter his knee and he'll drop like a stone."

MORE TIPS ON QUELLING A BARGUMENT:

1. **Swignore the problem.** Just shut up and drink.
2. **Extend the olive branch.** Buy him a martini to remind him you're his bro. Just remember to cheers him or there'll be a bargument about what a rude bastard you are.
3. **Enter into a chugreement.** Agree to chug your next drinks. By the time you reach the bottom of them he'll be **ginoculated** and will forget what the hell you were barguing about.
4. **Create a pisstraction.** Getting up to drain the vein gives you time to cool your head and not be so pissed off. Just make sure you don't leave the table while he's talking or he may take the piss as a dis.
5. **Google it.** Tempers often flair when you and your bro disagree about obscure sports stats, or whether or not your bro is quoting *Tombstone* accurately. This is why you should get Google mobile to make sure you can always look up the correct spelling of porn star Spantaneeus Xtasty's name.
6. **Don't dis his sis.** When your bro is drunk, avoid any mention of his sister, his mother, hell even the lady who cleans his undies at the laundry.
7. **Avoid dumbbacks.** Don't even think of issuing ridiculously

dumb comebacks like "Not!," "Whatevs," "As if," "Eat me," "I know you are but what am I," "Talk to the hand," or throwing up a W hand sign to indicate "Whatever." Any one of these are the equivalent of slapping a "PUNCH ME" sticker on your jaw.

8. **Nipple cripple or incap-ass-itate him.** Sometimes using logic on your bro will only further his desire to beat you down. Instead of trying to make him see reason, make him see the ridiculous rack on the chick that just walked in.

9. **Flip his narcisswitch.** Angry drunks usually have a switch that can be flipped to bring them back to normal. Appeal to his ego by encouraging him to share a favorite manecdote. "Dude, remember that time you ate twenty hot dogs and puked on the kid in front of you?"

10. **Hash it out.** By smoking up, of course. Unless someone is a **grasshole** who's a prick even when he's high, it's amazing how quickly he'll go from having a bargument to engaging in a mild-mannered, perfectly harmless **bongversation** about how Pink Floyd's *Dark Side* is the best album ever.

Follow these simple rules and whatever beef you're having will soon be firewater under the bridge.

flaccid rain – Hard liquor that makes you go soft, or brews that cause **beerectile dysfunction**.

flow-carb diet – A diet that consists of letting carbs flow into your body via booze and brews.

freebauchery – Debauchery that costs you nothing.
You have a drinking problem, and it's this: How are you going to pay for the massive quantities of booze you suck down? It's always good to show some **bingeinuity** and find free and creative ways to get smashed. Below are some options.

SOURCE OF FREE BOOZE	ADVANTAGE	DISADVANTAGE
2-for-1 happy hour special	Readily available every day of the week.	You have to buy one to get one.
An open-bar party	Makes your date think you have class and status.	Dirty looks when you start burping "Ludwig van Belchtoven's Fifth."
House party	You can bring a bottle of Two-Buck Chuck from Trader Joe's and then partake from the 28-year-old Highland single malt someone else brought.	These get lamer as you get older. At twenty-one, it's all about naked Twister. At thirty-one, it's all about baked Triscuits.
Looting a liquor store	Anarchy, chaos—even better than a mosh pit.	Getting tased and set upon by snarling German Shepherds. Even worse, your mom seeing you on the news.
Going to some chick's house and splitting a bottle of her wine	Corkscrewing her.	Grape juice makes for lame drinking stories. Not impressive to say you "killed a bottle of 2004 Carol Shelton Vineyards Zinfandel and then banged her."
Doing a "grave crawl" and digging up bottles that were buried with your guydols GG Allin, Frank Sinatra, etc.	Fixing yourself a "Corpse Reviver No. 2" cocktail with actual corpses nearby.	Gas costs; bottles might require extensive disinfection.
Crashing a wedding	Horny bridesmaids.	When you pass out face down in wedding cake, no one knows who you are or how to get you home.

gramouflage – Something used to camouflage a gram of coke: "A baby powder bottle is the perfect gramouflage. Unfortunately my sister came over and used mine on her kid and I ended up having to snort blow off of a toddler's ass."

Halley's vomit – A vomit comet the likes of which you see once in a lifetime.

kegulations – Regulations that apply to a keg or kegger—for instance, "There will be no **Easter kegs**—kegs that you hide from the rest of the party for easy access."

MC Hammered – The state of being so drunk that you forget that you're a white dude and you start thinking you can dance or act gangsta, when really you're a poseur like MC Hammer.

Certain VIPs—"Very Inebriated Persons"—blow some Benjamins on a bottle of bub in the club and suddenly they become cheap imitations of 50 Cent. They shoulder bump each other and yell, "Yo, you my boy!" Things get worse when the DJ starts spinning hip-hop and they rap along to lines like "I got

99 problems and a bitch ain't one," oblivious to the fact that "99 Luftballons" is more their speed. Eventually they become truly MC Hammered and bust out dance moves that, ironically enough, are so frightening they would turn a black man white.

When booze gets into the system of these Caucasians, it's like chocolate syrup going into a tall glass of milk. They'll jump into a breakdancing circle oblivious to the fact that doing a coin drop into a windmill is almost impossible in a three-piece suit. Or they'll approach someone five times their size and say, "You want a piece of this? Step to me, bitch!"

When your bro is MC Hammered, do him a solid and pay one of the bouncers to put him in his place by telling him, "What's up, vanilla face?" If he *still* insists that he's 2 legit 2 quit, there's not much you can do except distance yourself from him and make fun of his ridiculous Al Jolson act to the hot waitress.

neanderbrawl – A brawl that occurs among drunken neander-thals.

Booze very often acts as assholine by fueling asshole behavior. Someone with enough of it in his tank is bound to feel the "call to brawl." A bargument that turns heated will usually end in **fistibluffs**—to paraphrase Shakespeare, douchebags creating sound and fury signifying nothing—but occasionally it actually escalates into a classic bar spar and then inevitably becomes an outright neanderbrawl. If absolute chaos erupts in a bar, remember which weapons you have in your barsenal:

bloodweiser bottle – A bottle of Bud smashed against someone's bloody skull.

spar stool – A bar stool hoisted by the legs and used either to keep someone at bay or to hammer him in the head.

lemon/lime mace – A lemon wedge sprayed in an aggressor's eyes in order to disorient him so you can bring the Bloodweiser bottle down. Or pepper spray them by dousing Tabasco sauce in their eyes.

floormaldehyde – The sticky barroom floor can hold people in place while you beat them.

spray gun – A tonic dispenser sprayed in the face of a rival in order to disorient him, and then wrapped around his throat to strangle him.

shotglass put – A shot glass that you hold against your neck while twirling around, then launch at someone on the other side of the room.

gincendiary device – The classic Molotov cocktail, or "dirty (martini) bomb." Use it only if you're up against the entire bar and your only option is to set the place on fire and become a **barsonist**.

cueiville slugger – A pool cue swung across someone's face like it's a baseball bat.

palcohol – Alcohol that's acceptable to consume with your pals—the opposite of **galcohol**.

Look, on a first date it's fine to drink a Harvey Wallbanger if you plan to bang her against a wall. But when you're boozing with the boys, avoid pretentious cocktails and make it a brewski, just for you-ski. When ordering at a bar, ask yourself, WWRJD—What Would Ron Jeremy Drink? The answer is *not* a mojito or a chocolate martini or (God forbid) a pomegranate cosmo.

Sadly, though the martini is loaded with gin and was once a dude's drink, ordering anything that ends in "tini" is now **manathema**. If you *must* have a martini, order a Gibson whenever possible—it contains pickled onions instead of olives, and pickled things are manly.

Lite beers are obviously out of the question. If you order a Shamstel Lite, don't be surprised when your friends bust your balls the second you crack the bottle. The one exception here is Coors Lite. Why? Because it's the silver bullet. 'Nuff said.

WASTED WORDS

gutterly wasted – Passed out in the gutter.

frathoused – As shithoused as an entire frat house.

Hasselhoffed – You can't even pick up the cheeseburger you so desperately crave.

hitshammered – You can't articulate the word "shithammered." (Also: *hitshoused*.)

pankled – Your pants are around your ankles.

slammedicapped – You can't do the most basic things—you have to ask your bros to reach into your pants to pull out your car keys for you.

spintoxicated – Intoxicated to the point where stuff starts spinning.

Soy sauced – You forget Spanish isn't your first language and you tell someone, "Soy sauced" ("I am sauced").

three shits to the wind – You just crapped yourself.

transvestanked – You don't care whether the hooker you just picked up is a man or a woman.

As a rule, it's always extra-effective to use rhymes when describing your state of drunkenness: queasy and uneasy, smashed and trashed, sauced and tossed, shredded and breaded, in flight and out of sight, far gone with a hard-on, swerving and perving. You can even try the bluesman approach—"tore down, almost leveled to the ground"—or better yet, go for triple rhymes: Queasy, sleazy, and uneasy; smashed, bashed, and trashed.

pourizontal – Poised so that someone can pour beer in your mouth from above.

prebauchery – The party before the party.

Never use the word "pre-party"—as in "We'll be pre-partying over at Alpha Beta Asshat." This outs you as a rank amateur, since everyone knows that life is one big party and "pre-partying" is ontologically impossible.

Instead, refer to prebauchery, the partying equivalent of taking leisurely swings in the on-deck circle. Prebauchery might entail drinking some quiet beers at your local till you're buzzed enough to walk into the pants-off dance-off with your heads held high. Or it can also refer to debauchery that occurs before a sober act—e.g. "It won't look good if we flask it at the funeral. Before we head over to the funeral, let's engage in some prebauchery at Futtbuckers."

rebauchery – To participate in further debauchery the morning after excessive drinking.

> GUYKU #2
> *Stole a stuffed horse head*
> *Bar looking empty these days*
> *I'll drink to that shit, good times*
> —DANIEL RICCIATO

roundhog – A bro who greedily hogs the rounds that other people buy for him, but burrows deep underground when it comes time for him to reciprocate. If he does this specifically with Budweiser, he's a **'weiser miser**.

When it comes to drinking, certain types generously make **slurchases** for all of their bros. These are the real paltruists. For all of their generosity, they often end up having to close out their savings accounts while they close the bar, and they're left with no choice but to convert to **tabstinence**—the religious refusal to open up a tab because you know it will end in disgrace.

On the other side of the proverbial coin is the cheap bastard that literally tips the bartender in nickels and dimes. This dude figures out exactly what you owe by becoming **Barchimedes**—the bar version of the great mathematician Archimedes. He insists on getting cash from you, oblivious to the fact that the only time you should "go Dutch" in a bar is when you opt for Heineken.

When you're drinking with friends, don't be a **Henny pincher**—don't ask your bro to cough up an extra couple of bucks because his Hennessy costs a bit more than the well variety. Let it go, bro. Putting an extra two dollars on your tab ain't going to kill you, unless of course you're packing a **shred-it card**—a credit card that's so maxed out the barkeep will probably end up shredding it.

slurchase – A purchase made while you're drunkenly slurring your words. These usually spark calls from your credit card company when they see you spent one thousand dollars at a place called Jiggling Piggies and they don't recognize your drunken signature. Just tell them, "Don't worry, that's just my **blottograph**."

sobriepee – A piss that helps you determine your level of sobriety.

Walk into a bar's relatively quiet and well-lit bathroom and you'll probably realize you're DTIT (Drunker Than I Thought): One look at your beet-red face, untucked shirt, and dangling mouth in the mirror is enough to drive you to a tall glass of water. The real test, though, is whether you can take yourself out of your pants without soaking yourself, and whether you can make the bowl rather than **pissinfecting** everything in sight. When you have an overwhelming urge to spray "as far as the guy can pee," chances are that when you return to the restroom it'll be to slip in your own piss puddle and puke all over yourself.

speakquilibrium – The ability to speak without slurring your words. "Dude, don't call in sick for work until you get back your speakquilibrium."

the stripping point – Somewhat like the phenomenon explored in Malcolm Gladwell's *The Tipping Point*, the stripping point is the precise moment at which shots of Jäger cause a chick to want to get naked with you.

swignominius – Shameful due to one's inability to swig alcohol like a man: "Dude, you puked before making bar par? You should be deeply ashamed of this swignominius behavior."

throngversation – A conversation in a loud, crowded bar.

At any given bar, the douchecibel levels are so friggin high that it's impossible to hear yourself talk, much less the person you're screaming into the ear of—but that's a good thing. If it weren't loud you wouldn't have exchanges like the following:

YOU: "So what do you do?"
HER: "Did you say 'SLUT, let's SCREW?'"
YOU: "No, I said, 'WHAT do you DO?'"
HER: "Sure, I'd like to go screw."
YOU: "Uh . . . Okay!"

You'll often find yourself in a **Lil Jonversation**—in which you can't really hear the person you're rapping with so you just say "WHAT!," "OKAY!," "YEAH!" a lot, like Lil Jon. As annoying as this is, you know that if "Welcome to the Jungle" *weren't* turned up to eleven, you'd have to carry on normal conversation with the girl—which might lead to tense revelations that, for instance, you don't share political views, or for that matter that you don't really *have* political views or don't know the name of the current president. When you're talking to dudes, however, sometimes you do actually want to be heard, which is when you should retreat to the sometimes quieter beer pong room for a spot of **pongversation**—conversation that occurs over a game of flip cup.

Trojan whores – Hot chicks that you hide amidst in order to get into a club: "The doorman wasn't going to let us in but we told these Trojan whores we'd buy their drinks all night if they took us in with them."

3

PLAYER PALAVER

(n.) Palaver that is used by or about a total player.

Many words have been used to describe the player: cad, rake, swinger, womanizer, manwhore, playboy, pick-up artist—the list is almost as long as the list of chicks Derek Jeter has banged. A few men have even single-handedly added to these words: Giacomo Casanova lost his virginity to two sisters when he was just a **teenieboffer**. Don Juan killed the father of one of his conquests and then taunted the man's ghost. And Lothario's womanizing got the married woman he hooked up with so riled up that she offed herself.

Every modern-day Lothario, Casanova, and Don Juan dreams that his name, too, will someday be used to describe the players that come after him, which is why people in the seduction community operate under **screwdonyms** like Mystery and Style and come up with catchy terms like kino and peacocking. Until recently, these words were only used by bros in the know, and the strategies they described were extremely effective. Now, however, when you make fun of a girl's pit purse she just asks, "Are you negging me?"

Obviously it's time to add a few more entries to the playbook.

approxidating – Dating someone who is an approximation of another person, sometimes known as a **doppelbanger**.

You can't always get what you want, but if you try sometimes you might just get a girl with a similar cup size and hairstyle, and sometimes that's all you need to help you get over a hopeless obsession. Just make sure you don't go to too much trouble searching for a "body double."

THE APPROXIDATE BOILERPLATE:

Who To Approxidate`

1. **Porn stars and movie stars.** If Princess Leia still makes you want to pull out your light saber, jump on Nerve.com and search for Carrie Fisher in case she's someone's "Celebrity I Resemble Most."
2. **Ex-girlfriends.** The quickest way to get over an ex is to bang someone who looks like her but has bigger boobs. Just don't be too obvious when you post on Craigslist: "Looking for 7'2", half–North Korean, half–South Korean who makes a mean gumbo."
3. **A coworker.** It's hard to get ideas across when you're just waiting for your boss to uncross her legs. Nail her doppel-banger and all nervousness will evaporate—she'll think the winks you're giving her are a sign of confidence and collegiality, when really you're saying, "I've pretty much seen you naked."

Who Not To Approxidate

4. **An ethnic fetish.** If a woman in hijab gave you an amazing blow job, resist the temptation to **ginaralize**—don't hang out at the mosque yelling "Hollah!"
5. **Your best bro's girl.** If you're dating someone who looks like her but is uglier, the message is clear: You'd take your bro's girl at the first **coppertunity** (an opportunity to cop a feel). And if you're dating a hotter approximation, you're challenging your bro to steal her.

6. Your mom. The Freud dude was clear about this one.

Of course, you don't always have to go to such extremes to get a girl out of your system. Sometimes it's enough to **approxibate**— wack it to a photo of someone who looks similar. If you were recently dumped by a Pak with a big rack, just Google "Pakistani+tatas" and there you go—a *Rakistani* right at your fingertips!

arranged bedding – When your friend sets you up on a blind date with a sure thing, usually by showing a girl your MySpace page and telling her how loaded you are and how much you love animals.

bag and release – To bag a chick and then release her back into the dating pool; to hump and dump.

battleshipping – Attempting to pick up a chick by hitting on every girl in the room as if you're playing Battleship.

Sometimes a cruising mission is like a game of Operation—you go into the bar knowing exactly who needs to be picked up. When you operate on them you have to be careful not to upset the elements around them (possible boyfriends, jealous friends, etc.). Nobody's nose will turn red if you botch it, but your balls *will* turn blue.

Other times, however, the bar is a vast sea of **pussibilities**, and you just launch into all-out **whorefare**, firing indiscriminately in hopes that you'll eventually hit a vulnerable target. Sure, you'll be launching missiles into the Pacific at first, but eventually you'll nail that Destroyer that goes down after just two tequila shots.

bitchhiking – Standing around like a hitchhiker, waiting for chicks to pick you up.

Scoring usually takes a **hoactive approach**, but sometimes you just sit back and let 'em come to you. If you aren't a rock star and don't have roadies hand-picking groupies, here are some poses you can strike that will cause girls to flock to you like shit-happy pigeons to a statue.

1. **Rodin's "Drinker."** Slumps over the bar with his chin on his fist as if he's lost in thought, until someone asks, "Why do you look so serious?" **Follow-up line:** "You don't like being taken seriously?"

2. **The Bookworm.** Sits around pretending to read **cliterature** such as *The Lovely Bones* until someone asks, "Are you liking that?" **Follow-up line:** "Not as much as I'm liking *that*" (points to her ass).

3. **The Lilith Fairy.** Goes to lesbian folk-singer concerts until someone asks, "Is this your first time seeing the Indigo Girls?" **Follow-up line:** "I'm a big fan. Actually I have a bootleg of their first show back at my place . . ."

4. **The Downward Horndog.** The only dude in the yoga class; waits for some girl to say, "Could you help me stretch?" **Follow-up line:** "What are you going to do for *my* muscle?"

5. **The Marlboro Man.** Stands outside of the bar smoking until someone asks him, "Do you have a light?" **Follow-up line:** "Clearly *you* do, because you just lit up my life."

6. **The Fag-Hag Stag.** Hangs out at the gay bar until a girl who's there with her gay best friend asks him, "Are you gay or straight?" **Follow-up line:** "If I was gay before, I'm hetero now."

7. **The Tourist Trapper.** Hangs out in a tourist area until some hot French chicks ask him, "Where's the metro?" **Follow-up line:** "The subway's dangerous—hop in my car and I'll take you to the hottest spot in the city. It's called My Place."

8. **The Sommelplayer.** Hangs out in the wine aisle at the supermarket until a MILF asks, "Excuse me, could you recommend a good red?" **Follow-up line:** "None of these wines have aged as nicely as you have."

9. **The Tallboy.** Hangs out near shelves where there's a chick item on the top shelf until someone says, "You're tall, could

you grab that for me?" **Follow-up line:** "Sure, as long as you grab *this* for me" (pointing to his junk).

10. **The Floor "Worker."** Hangs out at a store, dressed vaguely like an employee, until someone asks, "Excuse me, do you work here?" **Follow-up line:** "No, but I do work *there*."

blow for blow – An instance of blowing money in order to get blown—called a "pound for pound" in Britain.

Blowdysseus – A dude who is willing to go on a ten-year journey just to get blown: "No way am I going home just because it's 4 a.m., dudes. I'm Blowdysseus tonight. I'm willing to battle a Cyclops for the sake of *my* Cyclops."

boffice – 1. A place where you do your dirty work with a girl, boffing her like you're getting paid for it: "Would you mind stepping into my boffice? This'll only take a few minutes." 2. Term used for the office when you're boffing a coworker

Ah, the office life: Day after tedious day of going in and out of revolving doors, in and out of Excel documents, and in and out of client meetings. Who can blame the man whose mind turns to the ol' in and out? Why populate spreadsheets when you can copulate on top of bedsheets? Closing that deal with the Japanese takes months of negotiation, dozens of lawyers and accountants, and several cross-continental flights—whereas closing the deal with the new marketing assistant takes just four shots of tequila. And just like that, you've got a **bofficemate**.

Many are the repercussions of turning a colleague into a **balleague**. For one, your boss might pick up on it when you actually come to work smiling in the morning, get jealous you banged his assistant before he did, and increase your work load to insure that you spend the rest of your days filing memos instead of defiling bimbos.

Of course your coworkers are also going to envy you for "getting a leg up"—they'd probably trade their 401(k)s for the secretary's double Ds. Before long, you'll find yourself ignored at meetings, condescended to by colleagues, and talked about behind your back—which is pretty much how it was *before* you started hitting the receptionist, so by all means play on, player, play on.

The best way to determine whether it's worth getting with a coworker is by doing a "T&A P&L"—a calculation of profit and loss that pertains to tits and ass.

Consider these variables: Does she work on a different floor or at least on a different side of the building? +1. Is she your superior? −1. Is she the hottest girl in the office? +1. Is she good friends with the hottest girl, meaning if you do her you might be blowing your chances with the hottest girl? -1. Would she be into a threesome with you and the hottest girl in the office? +50. When you look on her desk, do you see a framed photo of a boyfriend who looks like he could throw a Xerox machine onto your head? −50.

bongquistador – A dude who somehow conquers hot chicks despite being a total bongsucking pothead. He gets the job done by **baking and entering**—smoking a girl out till she's so out of it she smokes him.

clockblocked – Not being able to initiate or complete sex due to a time constraint.

When a girl looks at her watch, you realize the game clock has run out on your cock. You wonder why you spent the entire date making inane chit chat when you should've been asking her deeper questions like, "Are you a squirter?" The tendency here is to throw a **Doug Booty**—a Doug Flutie–style "Hail Mary pass" made at a woman at the last second. Sometimes these passes connect—nine times out of ten they bounce in the end zone. But there *are* some moves you can try when it's clear that she's ready for the date to be over.

WHEN YOUR TIME IS UP:

HER PLAY	YOURS
Looking for a lifeline, she starts checking her text messages.	Text her something irresistible, like "You have beautiful eyes" or "Want 2 F U."
She invites you to the Bottom Feeder to meet her gay best friends, knowing you'll pass on it.	Agree to go, then one-up her by dancing with her friends. (Do not, however, accept their invitation to go to the Larry Craig Memorial Suite in the men's room . . .)
"Well, I have to get up early for work tomorrow . . ."	Tell a story about a work-obsessed friend who died on his way home after refusing to have another drink with you. Break down crying and then throw the Doug Booty while she's having another drink out of guilt.
"You know, it's a school night . . ."	Change the subject to a hot teacher ("Didn't you love Mark Harmon in *Summer School*?") and pray her horniness rubs off.

cock bottom – The low-point of your sexual career. "Dude, last night I hired a transvestite hooker. I was her last customer for the night so she changed out of her heels and into her Timberlands. Then she beat me with them when I didn't have ten bucks for a tip. I've hit cock bottom. I'm really 'gutter balling.'"

cock stock – The value of your penis to chicks.

Diamonds are a girl's best friend, but penises are also up there. Think of your cock and balls as stocks and bonds. Their value to women fluctuates based on a number of variables. If your cock stock plummets, you can bet girls aren't going to go down on you. Take this survey to see whether you'll have chicks clamoring for you like coked-up traders on the exchange floor.

CALCULATE YOUR COCK STOCK:

You just spent a week in:

Bali	+1
Baltimore	-1
Baltimore City Jail	-2

For breakfast you eat:

On the French coast	+2
French toast	+1
The French toast, bacon, egg, and cheese sandwich at Burger King	-1

You have a fat:

Wallet	+1
Ass	-1
Wife	-2

You speak:

Four languages	+1
Klingon	-1
To voices in your head	-2

The most expensive thing you own is a:

Mercedes S-Class	+1
Microsoft X-Box	-1
A box of XXX vids	-2

Your credit card is:

Amex Black	+2
Amex Gold	+1
Maxed	-1

When you say "favorite driver" you mean:	
Chauffeur	+2
Golf club	+1
NASCAR racer	-1

6–10: Congratulations, you're a hot commodity on the NAS-DICK exchange.

0–6: Hang in there—the market might turn.

0 or below: Blue chips? Try blue balls.

Craigslust – Lustful feelings as pertains to Craigslist.

Ah, Dregslist—the murky sediment of the dating pool. Just like porn, it caters to whatever freakish fetish you're under the sway of at a particular moment (a quick search for "milfy midget" *et voila*) but unlike porn you're dealing with actual people who might end up going apeshit on you, or at the very least making everyone in the restaurant snicker when you meet up for the blind date and "full-figured" turns out to mean she weighs four figures.

When experiencing Craigslust, jack yourself before you wreck yourself. If you give yourself a **reality jack** and it still feels like a good idea to take out that evangelical Christian who's looking for someone to spend the apocalypse with, then go ahead—click and dick!

cruiseapalooza – An exceptionally cruisy situation: "The girls in there were eyeing me like I was the last bon bon in the box. It was cruiseapalooza, man. I felt like the mayor of Ginatown."

cuddle shuttle – The taxi that takes you back to your **scoremitory**.

cupgrade – To upgrade to a girl with a bigger bra size: "Jen's cool but she's a double B. I need to cupgrade."

dick-up line – A line you use after a successful pick-up, to see if she wants to take it to the next level. A lot of players make the mistake of issuing the dick-up line *instead of* the pick-up line. They'll ask a random pedestrian, "Yo baby, you wanna get with me?" Even if she's dressed in **ho couture** and seemingly ripe for the dicking, you have to lead into this gently. Stop her and ask her for the time. Then say, "Yo baby, you wanna get with me?"

digit midget – A dude who gets tons of digits despite his midget-like height.

Small guys often get the short end of the dick, but some are endowed with such confidence that they could go head-to-head (well, head-to-knee, anyway) with Wilt "The Stilt" Chamberlain in a digit-gathering competish. First and foremost among these nutting Napoleons is Kim Jong-il, who at just 5'5" is a much feared launcher of flesh missiles. He has fathered no fewer than eleven kids and employs a "pleasure brigade" that dances naked the moment he snaps his child-like fingers.

Of course, not all short dudes have the luxury of inheriting a country—much more common is the pint-size player who joins Nerve.com and becomes a regular **Nervé Villechaize**, seducing girls online with an outsized personality to such a degree that they overlook the guy's pygmy-like stature when they meet him.

drillosophy – A philosophy about drilling chicks, for instance: "Hit it, quit it, and pretend you never did it."

Skintellectuals dedicate their every waking hour to pondering **sexistential dilemmas**. History is full of these "great dinkers":

Mackiavelli – A prince of pussy who believed in getting some by any means necessary, and that "all's fair in love and whores."

Plato's Retreat – Posited that if you were stuck in a cave and the shadows of fugly chicks were the only thing you could see, you'd want to hook up with them.

Cockrates – Asked a series of questions in order to convince a girl of his initial hypothesis that she should get with him.

Splaycartes – Believed "I dink, therefore I am."

Whorin Kierkegaard – A sexistentialist who believed in taking care of #1 first.

Hegel of Keigel – Advocated a dialectic that involved taking a thesis ("You want to have sex with me, don't you?") and an antithesis ("I don't want to have sex with you") and developing a synthesis ("Okay then, blow me").

Long-Cock Rousseau – Believed there was a "social contract" that obligated women to blow him.

fish dish – A plate that you only make for girls, when you're fishing for R. Kelly–style "sex in the kitchen"—often the one thing you know how to cook.

flabotage – An act of sabotage that occurs when someone pushes the fat girl on you: "Chuck totally flabotaged me by asking the hot one to play air hockey with him. I got stuck with the **strippopotamus**."

flawthority – One who acts like an authority about a chick's flaws.
    When you're considering hooking up with a girl, it's only natural to think to yourself, "I wish I could cupgrade her to a C," or "If only her belly button was a second vagina," but why be so picky about dicking? There's no sense looking for a chick's **vag-ic flaw**: "I'd do her but she kind of has a unibrow." Hey, one eyebrow is better than none. Or, "She's built like a brick shit-house." Like it really matters when *you're* shithoused?

Chances are, your **spermcentile**—or the percentile of women you'd give it to—hovers around 70%, with that number going up to around 99.9% when you're at a club and down to about 15% when you're visiting a relative in a nursing home. The spermcenticle of **flawthorities**, however, usually hovers around 10%. Assuming only about 10% of that 10% of girls are willing to hook up, they're putting their odds of getting laid at 1 in 100. They're really shooting themselves in the dick.

Rather than stacking the bods against yourself, why not become a **flawportunist** and use a girl's shortcomings to get with her. Approach that chick with a unibrow and ask her if she happens to be Eastern European. Boom! Conversational fodder!

Flesh Direct – A **rendez-screw** where you don't have to go on a date with a girl or see her in the outside world—instead you get **whore-to-door delivery**. Setting up a **ho-to-do'** is as easy as having a nice couch, a bottle of **Whoredeaux,** and a TV that picks up **ho shows** like *The Hills*, *The OC*, or *Gossip Girl*.

When it's you who's showing up at her door, it's a **seedy delivery**.

flirtchase – A flirtatious purchase made for a woman in lieu of coming right out and saying you want to do her.

flirtuoso – A virtuoso when it comes to flirting.

freakquilibrium – Your natural state of freaking: "Man, I'm on a real **troll roll** right now—I've practically hit cock bottom." "Yeah man, you need to step up your game and get your freakquilibrium back."

ginasty – A man's dynasty as judged by the vaginas he has had. Wilt "The Stilt" Chamberlain has perhaps the greatest ginasty of all, having bagged twenty thousand chicks. The man is a real **ginamo** with a diverse **hofolio** and an overflowing **whorenucopia**.

Gump dump – When you dump a girl by assuaging her with trite clichés like "Life is like a box of chocolates" and then you run a thousand miles in the opposite direction.

Sure, sometimes you need to **Humpty dump** a girl by breaking up with her in such a cruel way that she'll never be able to pick up the pieces. You **Schwarzeneg** her by telling her "I'll be back" only to terminate relations with all the callousness of a cyborg. But more often than not, you'll want to let her down easy in one of the following passive-aggresh ways.

The Frump Dump – You stop attending to matters of *guygiene* and "let yourself go." She picks up on the hint that you just don't give a shit and next thing you know, she's gone too.

The "What A Dump" Dump – You take her to a shitty restaurant or your messy apartment to make her never want to see your cheap, slobbish ass again.

The "Down in the Dumps" Dump – You pretend to be so depressed that you can't leave the house or see anyone.

The "Dumping Your Problems" Dump – You bitch about your miserable existence until she doesn't want to deal with your pathetic ass anymore.

The Mumps Dump – You pretend to have an infectious disease that prevents you from seeing others.

The Data Dump – You mathematically prove why you shouldn't be together, e.g. "50% of marriages end in divorce," or "75% of women your age want to get married within two years whereas 85% of men my age would prefer an orgy with the Dallas Cowboys cheerleaders."

The Clothing Dump – You return all the clothing she left at your house as a hint that you don't really want her staying over anymore.

The Trump Dump – You dump her at a four-star **impresstaurant**, making it impossible for her to consider you a jerk because you just treated her to a five-hundred dollar dinner. Alternately, when you just point at her and say, "You're fired!"

harassanova – A dude who thinks he's a Casanova when the only reason a girl would ever go out with him is to get him off her crack. Sometimes known as a **sweet-stalker** because he refuses to stop sweet-talking girls, or a **Pepe Le Spew** because he follows girls like a skunk who's desperate to spunk.

Hittin'-this protection program – A program that allows you to hit it with a new girl without getting whacked by the last girl you dated.

Sometimes a girl you've dumped won't take no for an answer and demands to know why you can't be together4ever. She engages in "package tracking" to keep tags on your **pairabouts** (the whereabouts of your balls). You can't tell her you've moved on or you'd be sleeping with the fishes—and not in a good way. That's when you enter the hittin'-this protection program by calling upon your bros not to release any information about your current dating status, listing yourself as "single" on your social networking page, and sporting a faux handlebar mustache if it comes to that.

hog wild – A sudden, deranged, and often self-destructive appetite for fatties: "Dude has gone hog wild. The other night he was bragging that he pulled off something called a fat chick hat trick."

HONAR – A SONAR-like ability to know where the hos are at: "My HONAR is sensing a bachelorette party at Futtbuckers. Onward ho!"

honkystador – A total honky who conquers exotic chicks like Bowie bedding Iman.

horndogma – The dogma of a true horndog.

Horny bastards are often compelled to canonize their thinking about dinking. It doesn't matter whether they're Breastbyterians or they study the book of Booteronomy—they're determined to push their horndogma on anyone that'll listen. They'll open to the Book of Jobs and feverishly preach the virtues of HJs over BJs no matter how many times you tell them you're not a believer. They'll pepper their sermons with commandments like "once you go black, thou shalt never go back." The worst are the "porn-agains" who discover a favorite porn site late in life and feel the need to push it on you. When a horndogmatist prose-lytizes about prostitutes or sings a hymn about trim, gently remind him that sexual preference is a very private matter. Encourage him to be **perversatile**. And then go home and check out the website he recommended. Who knows, it might be worth the $19.95.

impresstaurant – A restaurant you take a date to in order to impress her.

When you're with a girl that you want to wine and dine and do from behind (they don't call 'em doggie bags for nothing), wow her by booking the chef's table and arrange a tasting menu of all the dishes that'll have her showing you her yum-o face—caviar, foie gras, sea urchin. If she goes for the one hundred dollar *fruit de mer* tower you can rest assured that oysters won't be the only thing she'll be slurping that night.

At an impresstaurant, the sommelier is both your wine man and your wingman, presenting bottles of Pinot Noir to you with a fancy cumrag draped over his arm. He's the oenophile to your boneophile—he describes the wine's body while you run your eyes all over *hers*. He hypnotizes her with winespeak like "fruity" and "nutty" while you think, "*I don't know about fruity, but it's about to get very nutty indeed.*" Just make sure he doesn't make you look bad—send back at least three or four bottles to show your date you know a thing or two about 1787 Chateau Lafite yourself. With any luck it'll become a regular thing and you'll become **foiegbuddies**—after treating her to some expensive foie gras you stuff yourself down her throat.

in-charge card – A charge card that puts you in the driver's seat: "No, we're not going to Vegan Vanessa's, we're going for booze and boobs at Hooters. I'm the one with the in-charge card." Guys who use their GlamEx on a meal sometimes experience a "signing boner"—they know that as soon as the bill is paid they're going to get laid. Even more impressive is when you pay in Benjamins—that's when you're a real **Cashanova**.

jiggy bank – A store of money that will cause a woman to get jiggy with you: "Once I get a few more ducats in my jiggy bank, I'm really going to be bringing home the bacon curtains."

landicap – A handicap that prevents an otherwise capable player from landing women: "He's a really good opener but he never seals the deal. He has a serious landicap."

last bitch effort – When you're kicking it to a girl who's your last chance to get into someone's pants—either because she's the only chick left at the bar or because you're too smashed to approach anyone else. When *you're* the only single dude left at the bar, you're the "last man landing."

lez dispenser – A dude who turns women into lesbians, usually via **malienation**: "His last three girlfriends ended up hating men and dating women. He's a total lez dispenser."

Mackiavelli – One who uses Niccolo Machiavelli's teachings to mack on chicks.

Forget the knight in shining armor—mackiavellis believe that the guy who gets the girl is the prince bent on achieving his ends by any means necessary. According to mackiavellis, the ideal player—just like the ideal ruler—is one who comes off like a nice guy but secretly uses a lot of **chickanery**—or misleading talk directed at chicks. Basically every 80s romantic-comedy villain was a mackiavelli—you know, the jock who the hot girl thought was a stand-up guy but was in fact a douche. The nerd in love with the girl knew this all along, but couldn't say anything, because he was afraid of a beatdown (as Machiavelli said, better to be feared than to be liked). In 80s movies, the mackiavelli is always outed in the end and his Porsche usually explodes in a fireball and he unsuccessfully tries to smother the fire with his prized letterman jacket that the girl has just thrown back in his face as she goes off with the nerd. Let's face it, though—life isn't an 80s movie. If it were, chicks would be wearing mullets and shoulder pads and there'd be no reason to hit on them in the first place.

There's no evidence that Machiavelli ever intended his rules of war to be applied to the battle of the sexes, but that's of no consequence to mackiavellis. This chart should help you understand how they operate.

WHEN YOU'RE ASKING YOURSELF THIS . . .	REMEMBER THIS . . .
Should I cheat on her with her best friend? Isn't that going to come back to bite me in the ass?	"People will seek revenge for minor hurts but will not be able to revenge major ones."
Should I be nervous that she's having a drink with this guy, even though she says it's platonic and he's "harmless"?	"It is a general rule about men that they are ungrateful, fickle, liars and deceivers, fearful of danger and greedy for gain."
Should I go to her friend's wedding like I said I would or stay in and watch the game?	"The promise given was a necessity of the past: The broken word is a necessity of the present."
We've gone out on five dates—should I maybe start paying for dinner?	"Benefits should be conferred gradually, and in that way they will taste better."
I'm stricken by guilt. Should I maybe confess that I went into her e-mail and told her ex-boyfriend never to contact her again?	"A man who wants to act virtuously in every way necessarily comes to grief among so many who are not virtuous."
Should I stop sneaking around on her, or keep sneaking around but just be careful to leave less whorensic evidence lying around?	"The man succeeds best who knows best how to play the fox. But it is necessary in playing this part that you conceal it carefully; you must be a great liar and hypocrite."

malienate – To alienate a woman with male behavior.

Chicks will put up with only so much before they vow to find a better man (and then convert to lesbianism). When a relationship goes south and you don't have the heart or the balls to say, "I once found you hot but now you're about as exciting as month-old hummus leftovers," one option is to devolve into a knuckle-dragging Simian, a strategy known as **Cavemanning**. Initiate a break-up of attrition: Ask yourself, WWJD—What Would a total Jerk Do?—and do it until she gets fed up with you. Just like the FBI piped non-stop Buddhist monk chants into the Branch Davidian compound to get David Koresh to surrender, you can play *Grand Theft Auto* at full blast until she decides she never again wants to hear "It's time for the Vance Lance Dance." *Voila*—you've gotten rid of her without having to feel guilty about dumping her, and (better still) after hours of gameplay you've finally found Vice City's hidden strip club.

HOW TO MALIENATE A WOMAN IN 10 DAYS

Sunday: Order a catering-size sub—don't offer her a bite until you're down to the last foot.

Monday: Start calling her "dude" and knuckle-bumping her instead of kissing her goodbye.

Tuesday: While she's going down on you, snap into a Slim Jim.

Wednesday: Ask if she wouldn't mind picking up your wallet from the strip club where you left it last night. "It's probably with this girl named Candy. Leave her fifty for a tip."

Thursday: Get her a birthday cupcake and when she tells you her birthday isn't for months, say, "Damn, must've been thinking about someone else." Eat it.

Friday: Be a **corn-dog horndog** by inviting her to "dinner and a movie"—a corn dog and a porno.

Saturday: Slay her with Slayer. When she tries to have a heart-to-heart during "Angel of Death," turn it down slightly, listen to her for about fifty seconds, and then turn it up twice as loud—"Drum solo!"

Sunday: Start leaving the toilet seat up. And stop flushing the toilet.

Monday: Throw her a "foul towel" that's been at the bottom of your hamper for a year.

Tuesday: Wipe feces on your face and tell her you're trying on your Halloween costume—"I'm GG Allin!" If that doesn't scare her off, nothing will.

manecdote – An anecdote that shows what a man you are.

Every player should have a go-to story that turns a girl to slutty putty. Whether you're busting it out on a first date to soften her up, or dropping one when it's time to close, make sure to have a few of these in your **prepertoire**.

1. **The Gulliver's Travelogue**—A story about your travels in a totally awesome foreign country. "It was Amateur Night at the bullfighting ring . . ."
2. **The "Daily Planet" Item**—A story that shows what a good Samaritan you are. "I couldn't just watch them steal her wheelchair . . ."
3. **The Creation Myth**—A cute or heart-wrenching story about how you were born: "I had to chew through my umbilical cord, or I would've died . . ."
4. **The Story of O**—Shows off your sexual prowess. "After her fifth orgasm, the priest on the other side of the confessional was like, 'Heavens!' "
5. **The Fairy Tale**—Shows her your sensitive side. "Actually, I took ballet when I was a kid . . ."
6. **The Sob Story**—Makes her go, "That's *so sad*." Sometimes

called a SOB story, since you're a son of a bitch for using the death of your grandmother to get pussy.

7. **The Momoir**—Shows how much you love your mom or how cute she is.

on-dick circle – The on-deck circle in which you keep the next girl in your **screw queue**.

palibi – Telling your girlfriend that you're out with your pals as an alibi. Sometimes called a "cock and bull" story.

Cheating can amount to **screwicide** unless you have a solid alibi. Let's say your girlfriend discovers whorensic evidence such as a No-Tell Motel receipt in your pocket. There's no dodging the fact that you were there, so tell her it was for poker night with your pals. If necessary, stall for time by saying, "I'm not sure I want to tell you . . . you might get mad . . ." This shifts her from the **ho-fensive** to the defensive. She'll have to promise to be cool with it, and probably *will* be when it isn't as bad as she thought it would be: "We rented a stripper for this guy Jason's bachelor party and I got a lapdance from her *while I was thinking of you* . . ."

But what if she doesn't buy it? You're going to have to make sure your bros are ready to cover your ass like a tight pair of Speedos. Don't, however, offer them up as witnesses—she'll only suspect you've coached them. Be reluctant—but not confrontational—when she starts demanding to talk to them ("I don't know about that honey—I guess I'm willing to do it, but I'm worried that they'll make fun of me for being totally whipped") and then finally break down: "Okay, fine, if it means *this* much to you."

Of course, you'll have to let your bro know that you're in need of back-up, for instance by pocket-dialing him during the argument so he knows what the palibi is (don't worry, he won't hang up when he realizes it's a pocket dial—as soon as he hears your chick tearing you a new one, he'll be laughing his ass off). Be careful who you pick as your witness—if your girlfriend is smoking hot, your bro may take advantage of her vulnerability and snitch on you to get her. You'll quickly find yourself stabbed in the back, saying, "*Et tu*, bro?"

Another possible blowback is that your pal goes way overboard. Make sure he doesn't tell your girl stuff like, "Oh don't worry, he'd never do that to you. He loves you. He even told me he wanted you to have his babies. He told me he wishes you would secretly stop taking the pill so he can father your child ASAP. Great, glad I could clear this up! Oh and FYI—he also says he likes to have his penis bitten during sex. Nice and hard."

Finally, don't **pass the fuck** by telling her it was your boy who cheated. The worse you make your witness look, the less likely he is to testify for you: Not even your best bromo will want to say that he cheated on his girl or hooked up with a fifteen-year-old.

Be reasonable and you can use palibis to get you out of a number of incriminating situations:

SITUATION	PALIBI	REASON SHE MIGHT NOT BUY THE PALIBI	SOLUTION
She finds a panty in your possession.	You went to a porn convention with your bros and bought Jenna Jameson's used underwear. You didn't want to tell her you blew $300 on it.	She can't find anything about the porn convention on Google.	Give her a friend's number and pay him to change his outgoing voicemail to "Undies of the Stars."
She finds holaroids of some naked chick.	Tell her they're photos of your friend's ex—you won them from him in a poker game.	The photos are on *your* digital camera. The one she bought you for Christmas.	Your pervy friend had to borrow your camera because the last chick he took photos of bashed his to pieces when he refused to delete them.

SITUATION	PALIBI	REASON SHE MIGHT NOT BUY THE PALIBI	SOLUTION
She reads booty texts that you sent to someone.	Tell her your boys had a bet going to see who could seduce this girl you all met at the bar. Your texts were just proof that you had the girl in the bag—far from planning to eff the girl, you intended to treat your girlfriend to dinner with your winnings.	She calls the girl you've been booty texting and the girl says, "Yeah, I effed him."	Tell her you paid the girl $50 to lie that she effed you—just so you could get the $200.
She actually sees you in bed with a woman.	Your bro, who's sterile, wants to have kids with his girlfriend and offered you $50,000 to inseminate her. You're only doing it for the money, and for your bro.	Your bro's check for $50,000 bounces.	"It seems he lost his life savings in Vegas last weekend, poor bastard. But he gave me an IOU. He's good for it, trust me."

pervception – The perception of a total perv: "Is it just my pervception or does that chick want to lick my bone like it's an ice cream cone? Because from my **pervspective** it looks like she does."

GUYKU #3
Spring out my ding dong
Piss in Japanese public urinal "soap land"
Got me rice for lice
—KOICHI FUJIMURA

pervsuade – To persuade a chick into doing something perverse.

pillsbury ho boy – A portly playboy who gets (or tries to get) tons of action despite his excessive party pudge.

Poinsexter – Someone who is well-sexed despite being a total Poindexter.

poondocks – The boondocks of poon, when you're far, far away from the slightest hope of poontang: "I have to go to my ex's birthday party—it's going to be the usual five fat chicks and their boyfriends, and it's at her house so there won't even be other chicks at the bar to hit on. I'm going to be out in the poondocks man."

Q & A.D.D. – When you ask a question but don't bother concentrating on her answer, because it's pure **vagibberish**.

A girl loves it when you ask how her day went. Unfortunately, her answer could take all night. After about four or five words your mind wanders, which is why smart girls just say, "It was okay I guess. How was yours?" leaving you free to entertain her with all the hilarious shit *you* did that day.

How does one overcome Q & A.D.D.? One option: Don't ask any questions, save for the occasional "Does this suit make me look awesome?"

roverdrive – An intense drive to hook up with a woman—any woman—no matter how much of a dog she is. This is called a **mutt rut** if you are accustomed to a higher caliber of woman but are temporarily hooking up mostly with dogs.

Guys will shift into roverdrive after about four drinks, and maximum roverdrive after about six. If her fugliness is a dog's only flaw, let your frothing friend take her to the pound, otherwise he'll wake up the next day and say, "Why did you cockblock me from that hot chick?" If, however, the dog displays evidence of mental instability (for instance, she tells your bro he reminds her of a boyfriend she just broke up with), it's possible she's a Cujo. Come to the rescue by warning the rabid dog that your bro has an STD—one that he doesn't know about yet since you (his roommate) just intercepted his test results in the mail. This will prevent her from questioning the friend about the supposed STD and outing you as a cockblocker.

scoregonzola – A pick-up line or method that's as cheesy as Gorgon-zola but somehow results in you scoring—sometimes referred to as **flirtilizer** because it's so full of shit. To pick up girls, you don't always have to be a **line-ocologist**, studying lines until you're Albert Linestein—sometimes you can just serve up some **hovolone** such as "Do you come here often? And how often do you cum?"

The put-down pick-up: When you "neg" her by telling her something like "Are you homeless? I think I saw that dress on *Project Runaway*."

The pompliment: When you compliment her in a pompous, arrogant manner: "I don't really dig blondes, but you have nice hair."

The barkeeper timekeeper: When you strike up a conversation with the girl who's waiting for a drink next to you by telling her that the bartender is slower than a retard stuck in quicksand.

The Jean-Claude Van Scram: When you threaten to kickbox the Harassanova who's hitting on her.

The fauxmosexual: When you act the part of a gay guy by telling her, "I love your hair. Have you ever thought of wearing it as a bob?" or "Ooooo, mind if I touch your boobs?" (The "oooo" is croosh.)

The two-against-fun: When you invite her to make fun of the losers on the dance floor.

The skevesdrop: When you start with, "I couldn't help but overhear . . ."

The Grey Poupon: When you ask her to borrow something, e.g. "Excuse me miss, are you using that salt shaker?" (cue "Rumpshaker").

scorgy – When you and your bros hit the club and it's a veritable orgy of scoring digits: "Dude, it was a total scorgy in there! We emerged **chicktorious!**"

screwmongous – Used to describe a boner so humongous it's fit for the screwing.

Sometimes you get a **Presidential erection**—a chub so big that "Hail to the Chief" starts playing. If you're walking around with one of these full-on robot chubbies you might call it a **pantler**, since it looks like there's a unicorn antler in your pants.

screw queue – An imaginary list of girls who might want to do you, ranked first to last according to when you plan to do them.

Channeling your **ho flow** is just like being an air traffic controller. To keep track of who is cleared for landing and which hos are in a holding pattern, you're going to need a "to do" list noting the quirks of each girl. Maybe one of them gets lonely on the weekends—sure, Friday is guy day, but keep her in the screw queue till a Friday night when you're keeping a low brofile. Maybe one of them only dates guys with money. Save her for the day you finally get paid for a big job and have some cash in your jiggy bank.

Screw queues are also useful when you're establishing **juris- dicktion** over a girl—letting your bro know who's on your **galendar** will discourage him from "ho poaching." Life isn't a porno where you and your boy can just perform a wobbly H on any girl you're both feeling. To insure a girl doesn't come between you (in the bad way), agree to a few **guydelines**—can you claim a girl simply by calling dibs and planting a "MINE" flag (Spermin' General's Warning: Don't actually do this—it might cause a UTI), or does she have to actually show interest in one of you first? And what's accepted proof of that interest? Be as specific as possible. You don't want to get into a sitch where you're telling your bro, "but she was into me first—she was always winking at me," and he tells you, "that's because I gave her a bad case of **dink eye**."

If the situation can't be easily resolved, you may have to make like Bonobo chimps and engage in some genital fencing. Turning your bro into a **bropponent** and engaging in **mantagonism** isn't ideal, but to paraphrase the Beastie Boys and the Red Hot Chili Peppers, sometimes you gotta fight for your right to party on her pussy.

Of course, good old-fashioned **dickplomacy** is always the best solution—negotiate for your right to make the move. Sometimes it's as easy as agreeing to finally tell your bro that cheat code for *Madden*.

senior clitizen – An old dog who is constantly looking for new tricks. Also known as Grandpa Spermin'.

slap shot – Taking a shot at a girl in such a manner that you risk getting slapped, for instance by saying "You remind me of the time I went door to door in the rich neighborhood selling candybars for my Little League team. The houses had really big knockers . . ."

spunk drunk – The perversion of reality that occurs during the afterglow of a **spracktacular** sex sesh: "Oh baby, I didn't mean it when I told you I loved you and wanted you to sire my progeny. I was just spunk drunk."

stalkward – Awkwardness that arises when you're trying to avoid a girl that's stalking you, for instance when you accidentally pick up a call she has placed on her "stalkie talkie."

stripper flipper – One who disarms and seduces a stripper, convincing her to give her real name and then giving her a ride home.

strongcharm – To strongarm a woman with your charm.

Sure you can passively wait for women to come to you, but you'll be much better off if you take control of the situation and strongcharm them into seeing things your way.

- Display an utter certainty that she wants you. You're attitude should be, "I'm totally jealous that you get to blow me tonight."
- Don't let her get the word "no" in edgewise. If you don't let her talk, she can't reject you.
- Be talky but not too cocky—keep the conversation focused on how **perb** you are but avoid outright **douchebragging**.
- Ask her about herself and then use her answer to let her know how awesome you are:

   "So where did you go to school?"
   "Sarah Lawrence."
   "That's amazing! My little sister's name is Sarah and she dated this guy named Lawrence! Actually he cheated on her

so I had to break his leg and feed it to him. So what's your favorite type of food?"

"Mexican."

"That's awesome. I had a Mexican girlfriend once. She loved dating a gringo because her ex was Speedy Gonzales, if you know what I mean. So what's your favorite color?"

- Be self-deferential but only in a way that indicates how ridiculously awesome you are: "It's so embarrassing, I only have one book in my apartment, Joyce's *Ulysses*. I was totally going to read it but I ended up cutting a hole in the middle so I could hide $75,000 in cash! I don't trust banks ever since they lost my last $50,000 bonus."

swivel dick – The boner you have (and sometimes point to) when you swivel around to look at the backside of a hot chick who just passed you on the street.

taparator – Someone who enters a tapas bar for the sole purpose of operating on the women.

The tapas bar is a classic breastination, partly because sharing food allows chicks to get together for dinner without actually having to eat (usually they invite one fat girl to hoover the entire table), and partly because they hope to meet a doppelbanger of the hot Spanish guy they hooked up with during their semester abroad. That's why there's even more action at a tapas bar than there is at a topless bar. The bartenders get more trim than anyone else on the planet—though if you ask to sniff their fingers, they'll probably just smell like garlic. Still, the guy who's ladling out the **bangria** doesn't have to be the only conquistador. You can easily use your knowledge of tapas to, well, tap ass:

1. **Don't be afraid to be cheesy.** It's your job to put the *man* in manchego. As soon as you overhear a girl asking one of her companions, "I wonder what the difference is between the

tetilla and the extramadura," be prepared to butt in and explain which one is soft and which one is, uh, semi-hard. (Note: *tetilla*, the soft cheese, means "small breast" in Spanish. Do with that what you will.)

2. **Ham it up.** "Pata negra" ham isn't available at many tapas bars—keep a stash of it in your apartment so you can invite girls back to taste your salty meat.

3. **Pose as a Spaniard.** Memorize a line or two of Spanish so you can pretend (while others are listening) to leave a phone message for another Spanish friend: "*Hola Jaime, soy Rodrigo. Estoy en el tapas bar, me puedes llamar? Quiero ser matador en la corrida de toros este domingo. Gracias, hombre.*" ("Hello Jaime, it's Rodrigo. I'm at the tapas bar, can you call me? I want to be a bullfighter in the bullfight this Sunday. Thanks man.")

4. **Say "see ya" to morcilla.** Avoid blood sausage. The *only* time a girl wants to see blood in your mouth is when you go down on her during her period.

5. **Likewise—gazpacho.** Think of Spain's national soup as "gas"pacho—the fatal combo of vinegar and olive oil will have you ripping game-killing farts during the crucial cab ride home. Sure, you can blame the cabbie, but then you'd have to slay the girl with your eye-watering garlic breath.

6. **Know your Almodóvar.** The chances that Pedro Almodóvar is the favorite director of a girl at a tapas bar are about equal to the chances that Jesus is the favorite deity of someone at a Catholic church. If you can make a solid thirty minutes of conversation about the man, you're good as New World gold. Make sure you claim to own all 139 movies Almodóvar has made, so you can invite her back to your place to watch whichever one she hasn't seen.

7. **Feign knowledge of the country.** Make it clear you've been everywhere in Spain that she has, even if you've never set foot in it—your favorite part was "hanging out in the plaza mayor" (that's safe—every town has a central square) and

visiting that beautiful church near the plaza mayor (also safe). And tell her you made friends with an old bullfighter.

8. **Make life richer with a pitcher.** Treating a table of girl-friends to a pitcher is the ultimate gentlemanly gesture. Hell, treat them to a pitcher of white, a pitcher of red, and a pitcher of rosé—who knows which one they'll prefer! By the time they're finished at least one of the girls will be good and hammered and you can approach the table with your line: "You're not going to eat the apples and oranges? That's the best part!" Note: You should have a bottle of beer in your hand as you say this. Only fruits drink sangría.

vadge of honor – A vagina you can be proud to have entered.

vagulation – Adulation received from chicks.

wee-rection – A wee erection you get, for instance, when you realize you're actually going to score.

God punished woman with painful childbirth and punished man by giving him unexpected boners every time he stands up to get off the subway. In a perfect world, you could use these "inappropriate displays of erection" as levers that open trap doors beneath you. Luckily there are easier things you can do to prevent erection detection.

1. **Create a chubstruction.** Cover up the chub with the nearest object. If a juggy jogger just gave you **G-spring**, slide the baby harness you're wearing down to your crotch area.
2. **Think of "downers."** Beat back your meat by picturing Mother Teresa surrounded by mosquitos and starving orphans. This won't work if you're picturing yourself banging a young, hot Mother Teresa.
3. **Picture a "death by hanging."** Picture the smallest weenis you've ever had, for instance when you suffered shrinkage after your ritual New Year's swim in ten degree weather.

4. **Uptuck it.** "It hides your boner and it feels awesome!"
5. **Engage in slacksturbation.** If someone is about to walk into the room and it would take less time to get off than to get turned off, just go ahead and cream your jeans.

whack-a-ho – When girls at the bar are just popping up at you one after the other and you have to decide which one to hit.

whoreography – The art of choreographing your ho flow so that the various girls you're hooking up with never know about—or bump into—each other.

whorenucopia – The array of women that you're attracted to or that are in play at the moment.

WINGLISH (N.) THE OFFICIAL LANGUAGE OF WINGING.

ball boy – A wing who gives you some much needed balls: "You're totally right man, that chick who looks like J-Lo *isn't* out of my league. Thanks for being my ball boy."

bonership (aka "bagging rights") – 1. Ownership you claim because you have a bigger boner for the girl than your bro does, or you had one first. If bagging rights can't be immediately determined, you may have to "draw dicks" to see who is harder up for the girl. 2. Ownership based on the fact that you're boning or have boned someone: "There shouldn't be a bone of contention here, man. I already hooked up with her so I have full bonership." Also called jurisdicktion.

galtitude – The altitude at which you and your wing are flying, based on the hotness of your targets: "Good news, bro, we're confirmed for the Ford Models party. We're going to be cruising at a very high galtitude."

gay cowboy – A gay wingman who occupies a girl's cowish friends while you hit on her. This doesn't actually have to be a gay guy, just someone who, like a gay guy, doesn't mind talking to heifers all night.

Greenpeace mission – An attempt to save a friend from harpooning a whale: "Dude, he's trying to Moby dick her. You better go on a Greenpeace mission."

hog tie – To tie up a porker in conversation so that your bro can hit on her hot friend (see **gay cowboy**).

pick-a-dick – When you both approach her with the agreement that as soon as she makes it clear who she's feeling, the other will back off. "Dude, I'm going to kick it to that girl." "No way man, I saw her first—I have jurisdicktion." "Okay, let's let her pick-a-dick."

post-game bro – 1. The bro you hang with after your game fails to get you laid, who tells you, "It's all right man, those girls were fugly buttslags anyway." 2. An instance of broing down post-game. "We had a post-game bro about the stuck-up bartender and how she acts like her clit don't stink."

rollmates – Guys who always roll together because they're soulmates when it comes to stuff like chasing chicks.

sacrifice fly – When you hold off on being fly so that your bro can score with a girl. An admirable act of **paltruism**.

troll stroll – When you play the **trollkeeper** by walking an ugly chick to the bar so that your bro can hit on her hot friend. A form of "jumping on the grenade."

zero cum game – A belief held by certain freakonomists that there is a finite amount of poontang in the universe and that if you're balling someone, your wingman must be getting blueballed. Though clearly a flawed theory unless you're sarging in an Afghan prison or you're at a party where the male to female ratio is similarly cock-shocking, the zero cum game can easily lead to a bargument—that's how much tension there is between the gets and the get-nots.

WINGMAN BROTOTYPES

THE BROTOTYPE	WHAT HE DOES FOR YOU
Murtaugh to your Riggs (aka "good cop, bad cop")	Makes you look valiant when you ask him not to interrogate her in such an obnoxious manner
Harry to your Lloyd	Even though you're dumb, he makes you look smart because he's dumber
Isiah to your Magic	Makes you look tall because he's a lil' midge
Hardy to your Laurel	Makes you look dapper because he's fatter than you
Garfunkel to your Simon	Makes you look like a rock star because he's so quiet and awkward
Oscar to your Felix	Makes you look like a sharp dresser because he's such a slob
Hooch to your Turner	Makes you look like a grown man because he's such a dog
Statler to your Waldorf	Helps you bitch about how lame the club is and how ugly all the chicks who aren't talking to you are

4

BANGUAGE

(n.) Language that pertains to banging a chick

Why is it that Salt-N-Pepa's song "Let's Talk about Sex" was heralded for its unprecedented frankness if it doesn't even mention a Dirty Sanchez? Obviously dudes are way better at talking about sex—from Shakespeare, creator of the word "undress," to the first dude who said "donkey punch." When chicks try to invent banguage, they just confuse everyone, like when Kelis referred to her "milkshake." Was she saying that dudes like sucking melted Ben & Jerry's off of her lactating titties? Probably, but who knows?

All told, two-thirds of male conversation revolves around getting laid. If guys didn't coin new words they'd be saying "vagina" more often than a gynecologist with Tourette's. Even variants like "pussy" get old, which is why we've come up with substitutions that are a lot classier, like "pink taco."

Who knows how many words comprise the **sexicon**—if you surveyed the back of the porno boxes in just one adult superstore and made a list of all of the **spewphemisms**, it would probably be longer than Lexington Steele's gushing flesh missile. But then why undertake something so tedious when you could be banging chicks and telling your boys about it?

At this point you're probably asking, "But what about that old rule—don't kiss and tell?" Well, that rule still applies. That's because kissing chicks is the gayest thing ever. Telling your bros you got a smooch is only going to make them wonder why the hell you didn't get cooch.

When you expound about pounding, take care to use words that don't make you look extra-virgin like olive oil. You'll come off like a total **nookie rookie** if you talk about "getting jiggy." Choose your words carefully or your bros won't think you're "telling it like it jiz."

Now let's get to the dick-tionary, shall we?

Arctic drilling – Drilling a girl who's a regular Frigidaire in the sack; laying Alaskan pipeline.

bang froid – Charlie Manson–like sang froid about banging a girl.

Let's face it, men do bad things: They kill, they torture, and in the case of Woody Allen, they do the truly unspeakable and play jazz clarinet. Another thing Woody did? He got with his old lady's adopted daughter and left holaroids of her lying around. Cold-blooded, but whatever: He ended up with Soon-Yi (giving new meaning to "Who's your daddy?") and did movies with Scarlett Johanssen, which proves that sometimes in life it pays to be a steely-eyed Sperminator.

It's not easy hardening your heart when you have a hard-on, but you have to be callous for the sake of your phallus. To be a "serial driller," you'll have to dump girls at Denny's like Jack the Ripper dumping them by the side of the road—you'll have to be the Joseph Stalin of ballin', the Charlie Manson of depantsin', the William Tecumseh Sherman of spermin', a regular Dirty Harry, asking your victims, "Am I getting lucky?" Just remember: Always go for the jugs, and don't shoot till you see the whites of their thighs.

bangover – The groggy, disheveled state you experience the morning after a night of excessive banging.

It sucks to go into the office with a hangover, but what about showing up with a *bang*over? This happens when you do the nasty into the wee hours and wake up in some chick's bed with mere minutes to get to work, meaning you have to completely neglect matters of **guygiene**. You pull a "rise and find" (locating your clothes as quickly and of course as quietly as possible—as the saying goes, "let sleeping dogs lie"), put on your dirty, rumpled clothes, and you make a run for the office while cursing the contact lenses that have been dry-humping your peepers all night long. You're so late that a trip to the ninety-nine-cent store to buy fresh tighty whities is out of the question, and you've gotten so little shut-eye that you don't realize there's a used Rough Rider stuck to the bottom of your kicks.

Don't expect your boss to give you a high five when you roll into work. Chances are *he* spent his night crunching numbers and he's going to resent you for spending yours knocking boots.

Here's how to mask a bangover:

1. **Give yourself a grinspection.** Before sitting in your cube, stare yourself down in the men's room mirror. Is your smile pube-free? If you have any hickeys or love bites, be prepared to explain.
2. **Sniff your stiff.** Your coworkers don't need to smell your smega. To freshen up on the fly, moisten a paper towel, squirt some pink soap into it, and boom! You've got an impromptu loofah.
3. **Don't go bragging about bagging.** You'll be tempted to send a **dickspatch** to your friends about your sexcapades last night, but don't get caught with your pants down. When it comes to company e-mail, waxing about trim can easily get you the "pink slip."
4. **Switch your britches.** Slip on the Polo jacket you keep in your office to take attention away from the Tom-Cruise-in-*Cocktail* shirt you're obviously wearing for the second day in a row. Make sure the jacket is covering up any and all **spewvenirs**—stains of the sort that ended up on Monica Lewinsky's blue dress.

banguine – Sanguine, or "happy-go-fucky," due to banging chicks on the regular.

Studies have shown that dudes who don't take their morning Blowzac are much more likely to fall into a deep depresh. On the other hand, the dude who gets blown as often as plays in *101 Sports Bloopers* walks around with a clit-eating grin, oozing confidence. And that's not *all* he's oozing, having just gotten a quick beej while everyone else was at the meeting. This man is gladsome—glad he's getting some. He is **effer-vescent**. He's quite gay, but not in a gay way. He feels like he's on top of the world, though he's only on top of a girl. He's on cloud 9, or maybe it's cloud 69? He's footloose and hopefully STD-free—

after all, even if you don't have a care in the world those warts might not have a *cure* in the world. And that's what's called a very "sad sack."

BLOWCABULARY (N.) THE VOCABULARY THAT PERTAINS TO GETTING BLOWN.

blowfessional – A highly headucated "blow pro" who goes down on you like she's getting paid for it.

blow jobligation – A chick's obligation to give you a beej. "Dragging me to her friend's party on a first date meant she had a hand jobligation, but as soon as I saw what Poindexters her friends were I told her she was blow jobligated, big time."

blowtivation – Motivation in the form of a BJ. "I can't start the day without some blowtivation. That's why I always insist on a 'cock-a-doodle-screw.'"

brainoument – The minute after a girl has given you head when she gazes longingly into your eyes and shows off the **cumbilical cord** that's still attached to her lips. A classic **pornsition**.

chapsdick – A dick that is rubbed on the lips like Chapstick. Slap it on her mouth and it's known as a **slapsdick**.

down grade – A grade that measures a girl's ability at going down on you, with F being Flaccid and A being Awesome!

eating jizorder – An eating disorder that's specific to cock-aholics: "I've never seen someone with such an eating jizorder—she was a total 'penis fly trap.'"

gagreement – A mutual understanding concerning whether she'll spit or swallow. When you tell a girl, "Put *that* in your windpipe and smoke it," you'll be tempted to shoot first and ask questions later, but if you commit **gaggrevated assault**, don't be surprised when you hit the "point of blow return."

Maxell – When you get head while you're leaning back in a comfortable chair, like the guy who got "blown away" in the Maxell cassette ads.

boomerwang – A wang that's curved like a boomerang, often seen in porn. Its owner is sometimes known as Captain Hook.

brawkward moment – An instance of adolescent awkwardness due to your inability to unhook or even begin to comprehend her fancy bra.

charity jerker – A girl who makes the ultimate **jackrifice** by jerking you off without asking for anything in return.

Getting a hand job is sort of like getting a bronze metal at the Holympics—it's simultaneously an honor and a disgrace. Still, sometimes a handy comes in handy: For instance when a girl tells you a **periodic fable**—a highly unlikely story about how she's on the rag so she doesn't want to have sex. At times like this, it's good to be with a girl who will beat your meat without asking you to grease her palm. It's not as hard as you think, since a lot of girls think of a jack-off as a write-off: They figure it'll come back to them. You have to hand it to a girl who's a sport about making you spurt. When she gives you hands-down the best handy of your life, you can't help but think, "Here's to women in the jerk-space!"

climaximum overdrive – The point just before you come when you start doing her in double-time.

clitastrophe – A fingerbang gone horribly a-dry, either because you're a **clitiot** and don't know your away around a vag or because the girl has a "flitty clitty" that's so hard to locate it's a regular Osama Bin Labia. If you don't have a high level of **cliteracy** and you find hers hard to read, ask her to lend a twirling hand. Otherwise you may end up in a **mosh clit** that's a chaotic and confusing miasma. Sometimes a girl is the only one who can show you around the **labiarynth**.

cocksmith – A "vagina miner" who can put it in a girl's keyhole with the exacting skill of a locksmith. To be a true cocksmith, you need to have a Cock of Gibraltar—a rock-hard skin flint that never goes soft on you. You need to be a regular Johann Sebastian Cock—a real "master organist." You need to be a "chief of staff," winning their hearts and minds via "cock and awe."

corkscrew – A screw that occurs at your apartment after you've uncorked a nice bottle of Hojolais. Sometimes referred to as "wining and dicking."

cracktivities – Activities having to do with a girl's crack, known as **spracktivities** if they involve busting a nut. "Dude, get out your 'sprack jacket,' this night is going to involve some illicit cracktivities."

cuddle scuttle – to flee post-coital cuddling obligations.

deja do – The haunting sensation that you've done this very thing while doing this very chick before.

If you don't want to see a girl again, it's probably because you don't want to experience deja do, a sensation that really gives you the booby jeebies. It's hard to define deja do. You could do a chick in the mish posish five hundred times, and if she's hot enough she still might not feel like ABC gum—"already been screwed." On the other hand, with a chick who isn't up to snuff when she's in the buff, you might get deja do the first time around—simply because she reminds you of every other boring boinging. To avoid deja do, add an element of surprise: Eat her out while she's sitting on an antique chair that could break at any second—known as a **wobbly gobble**.

dickinpox – A pronounced, chicken pox–like case of post-coital fever.

doorizontal – Doing it up against a door.

do-venir – A souvenir from a sex sesh.

Just as bullfighters keep the severed ears of the bulls they conquer, men often collect "chastity pelts." It starts in middle school, when you convince the first girl you finger to let you

keep her panties, and progresses till you're a grown man, pinning your used Magnums up on corkboard. Dovenirs are often gained by hook or by crook (plenty of dudes have secret recording studios under their beds) but beware: Chicks collect them too. Had Bill Clinton known this, he would've been more careful about putting his DNA on Monica Lewinsky's T&A.

drill pill – A pill such as Viagra that helps you give a girl a proper screw.

elephant-skin handbag – Your scrote, especially when girls use it as a "clutch bag."

erectectomy – An instance of something taking away your erection: "I was harder than Chinese algebra until her **haireolas** gave me an erectectomy."

floorizontal – Doing it on the floor.

gaz spaz – A woman who is a total spaz when she orgasms. Some girls have **sortagasms**—really quiet orgasms where you have to ask, "Did you come?" and she answers, "Sorta." But then there's the girl who's as vociferous as Margaret Higgins Sanger when you bang her. She's like Elizabeth Cady Pantin', preaching to everyone in hearing distance about a woman's right to come all night. Doesn't she get that you have neighbors who are trying to sleep? More importantly you have neighbors *that you're trying to sleep with*, and her nasty case of **Screwrette's** is totally blowing your chances. Or *is it*? When a girl participates in "ball and response," all she's doing is making it crystal clear that you're capable of giving someone a **floorgasm**—an orgasm that totally floors her. Don't be surprised when the next time you see your next-door neighbor, she asks you over for a spot of tea and then asks you to hit her spot of G.

gilingual – A dude who's really **tongue-ho** about getting a girl off; an expert **pube-a-diver** who can go down for hours without coming up for air.

ginamite – Anything that gets a chick to explode in uncontrollable arousal; pimp juice.

gropacetic – When a girl is copacetic with having your hands on her cans. "Dude, get a lap dance from the blonde one. I got one last time and she was totally gropasetic."

hardly-on – The quarter-chub that you get when you're hardly turned on; the opposite of a **tard-on**, a retardedly big hard-on.

holaroid – A Polaroid or other form of photo that depicts a naked ho you've banged. Known as **blowtographs** if they depict a hummer.

hornery – Ornery and horny at the same time. Used to describe someone who is "on the whorepath."

inspurt – To insert and spurt more or less simultaneously: "You're never going to be a world-class cocksmith until you learn to stop inspurting."

jack-n-pack – An instance of ejaculating and then immediately packing your stuff and getting the hell out of her apartment.

Sure it'd be nice if every time you did it with a girl you could stay over and wake her up with your "alarm cock." But sometimes you have to "take back the night" by getting some tail and then hightailing it out of there. Of course it's only right to offer an excuse when you hit it and quit it—tell her you need to check on your dog. If she catches you back at the bar where you met her a couple of hours ago, just say, "Like I said, I'm *checking on my dawgs* . . ." Chances are, however, she won't return to the bar since that would require showering and putting her makeup back on, which leaves you free to pick up another girl—maybe even one of her friends since by this time they'll be too wasted to remember which dude their girl went home with. This move is called "the Fireman," since you're pulling girls out of the bar, hosing them down, and then going right back into it.

jizaster – A jizzing related disaster. This can be used figuratively to indicate any dating-related **whoredeal**, or literally to indicate a disaster actually involving jiz, e.g. "I accidentally blew my load in her face and now she has 'dink eye.' It was a complete jizaster." When a situation is undesirable but unavoidable, one might say, "it jiz what it jiz."

johnsontration – 1. A girl's ability to concentrate on your johnson's needs while she's giving you a beej or a handj (referred to as **cuntsentration** if it's you focusing on *her* needs). 2. The concentration that you focus on your snow machine when you're trying not to make Christmas come early.

manpon – A male member that's so small that it doesn't go any deeper than a tampon would. Sometimes referred to as a **Planter's penis** because it is no larger than a peanut.

> GUYKU #4
> *Winter gale! Shrinkage!*
> *Sounds like a John Tesh album:*
> *"Intimate Windburn"*
> —SCOTT KENEMORE

narcijism – An undue fascination with one's own jism. Sure, your spunk contains millions of potential children, but you're not allowed to act like a proud father till an egg is actually fertilized. Don't go weighing your used condom on a fruit scale, and don't ask a girl if she's impressed by how far you fired your **jizooka**— you're in the bedroom, not at a shooting range. Even if you're a master blaster, avoid the temptation to tell yourself, "You've come a long way, baby . . ."

obestiality – The act of doing an obese chick like an animal.

Score a fit chick and you're likely to loofah her with a falafel Bill O'Reilly–style, lay her down in a bed of roses, and make sweet love to her while your boy Yanni tinkles the ivories. But get your paws on a *fat* chick and you'll go "hog wild." You'll get "mad cow disease" and do it "animal style" like you've ordered off the secret menu at In-N-Out.

If you're asking, "does obestiality really exist?" the answer is, "Does a five-hundred-pound bear shit Ding Dongs in the woods?" When you dig your spurs into a heifer who's heavy on the eyes, you're bound to last more than eight seconds—and there's nothing more ego-boosting than being able to do a chick till the cows come home. **Biggie bagging** is the best way to build stamina and to practice moves you're too insecure to try out on a skinny li'l thingie, so don't rule her out just because she looks like Jabba the Slut.

Oliver Twist – When you think you've given a girl enough but she begs, "Please sir, can I have some more?": "Jesus man, I took her to O-Town five times but she Oliver Twisted me into one last choregasm."

oraltruism – Oral sex given for altruistic purposes.

Sometimes it's good to show your heart is in the right place by putting your mouth in the right place. Go down on a girl without asking for anything in return and you're "in" for life (brownie points if it's her period). Sure, this sometimes leads to what is alternately called a boregasm (when it bores you out of your mind), a choregasm (when it feels like you're slaving away), or a snoregasm (when you all but fall asleep on her pudendum). Your endurance is tested to the point where it's an "Olympic chomp." But even if you've been going at it so long you've got a "touch of gray," remind yourself that you *will get by, you will survive*—and she might even pay you back with some "grateful head."

Be warned, though: It's not a charitable act if you ask for anything in the aftermath of the tongue tornado. It's a dick move to turn her afterglow into your pre-blow—kind of like giving to charity only because you're looking for a tax break. If you're absolutely incapable of oraltruism, there are ways to have your cake and eat it out too: While going at her, hang your legs off the end of the bed and stick your hard-on into the bed's "smack crack." She'll never know you used the mattress as a mistress.

By the way, when a girl does this to you, it's called "pro-boner work." You don't have to issue a "gag order" to get her to "give till it squirts"—just tell her, "Good things come to those who fellate."

x

orangubang – To bang her like you're a crazed **trimpanzee**: "I totally orangubanged this girl the other night—it was monkey see, monkey screw."

orgasthma – When a gaz spaz loses her breath as she gets off, causing you to wonder if you should reach for an oxygen tank.

pantique – A panty that has been lying around for so long that it qualifies as an antique. Such a panty has lost all sniffing value and is kept around only because you're pathetically ho-stalgic for whoever left it behind.

panty claus – A mythical figure who brings you presents along the lines of chicks in panties: "I got a visit from Panty Claus last night—this chick came up to me at the bar and just flat-out asked if I wanted to go home with her."

poonatic – A dude who's loony for poon.

poondoggle – An unnecessary or wasteful instance of scoring punani: "Dude, why did you hook up with Cindy? She's a total mutt." "Eh, don't even bring it up, it was a poondoggle."

popportunity – An opportunity to pop, usually one that shouldn't be taken.

When a girl gives you an out by saying, "it's OK, you finish," it's hard to tell whether she *actually* wants you to throw in the cum towel or whether you should issue an executive override and proceed to orangubang her. After all, maybe it's like earlier at dinner, when she told you to have the last bite of that really good dish and got mad when you actually ate it.

When a popportunity knocks, ask the girl a few times if she's sure she means what she's saying, just like a computer asking if you're sure you want to quit an application. Once *you've* shut down, there's no rebooting. Girls sometimes want to be talked into trying to come a third or a fourth time, just like they want to be talked into going for dessert at a restaurant. If she says "Well, mmmaybe," it's your duty to push on.

poptimistic – Optimistic that your night will "end with a bang."

pornsition – A position that would only be used in porn; it's so unusual it happens "once in a blue movie."

Obviously, porn is the most awesome thing in the world, but you have to be careful about **splaygiarizing** it. You've got real problems if you watch **earotica** and come off thinking it's okay to "ear plug" a girl. **Earjaculation** can cause serious hearing loss, even if you consider yourself a talented ear, nose, and throat cocker.

Pornsitions are usually invented by porn stars who get bored out of their minds going at it in the mish posish all day long, so to keep themselves from "balling asleep" they start thinking "outside of the box." The stuff they come up with is sometimes "Ball of Fame" worthy, but more often than not it's something Mother Nature never intended to have done to her.

The only time it makes sense to duplicate something you've seen in a porno is when the tracking is getting pretty bad on your favorite **titteotape**—in that case yeah, make a copy or two, or three, but generally you're usually better off **trimprovising**.

prepertoire – Your repertoire of moves that prep a girl to do it with you; your foreplay fortés. Foreplay has to be the biggest oxymoron since "softcore." The only time there should be a "fore" before "play" is during a round of golf. Nevertheless some women need to be "warmed up," and that doesn't mean turning up the heat in your hatchback while you do her in the back seat.

pussibilities – The possibilities for pussy: "Dude, this party is crawling with chicks. The pussibilities are endless."

ramnesia – Amnesia about ramming a girl.

It's one of the great guyronies that the drunker you get, the more likely you are to hook up with a girl, and yet the less likely you are to remember any of it. It's a disturbing form of "mammary loss": You try to remember sticking your face in them—"Did I do my booba diver routine?"—but nothing comes to you. A huge problem. If you can't even remember whether you actually did it or not, then you can't put the memory of it in your spank bank, or brag to your bros, or add it to your **gal tal** (your tally of how many gals you've bagged) unless you want an asterisk next to it Roger Maris–style. Obviously you're going to have to do a "do-over." Chances are you'll probably be just as wasted the second time you hook up with the girl, but this time at least you'll remember to turn on your spycam so you can make like an NFL official and review the tape the next day.

screwicide – Screwing a girl despite the fact that you know it's pretty much suicidal.

The French refer to the orgasm as "la petite morte" and indeed, sometimes it's deadly. Imagine your girl is coming home from work and you have this hot blonde in your bed. You want to go another round but you don't have time—and yet you're too horny to accept being clockblocked. So you take out your samurai sword and engage in ritual screwicide. When your girl walks in on you, you're balls deep, screaming BANZAI!

Given how much misery it leads to—the silent treatment, sexual withholding, constant reproaches, couples counseling, and in one notable case a presidential impeachment trial—it's hard to understand why anyone would engage in this sort of daring do. Are those five seconds of getting off really worth it? Shit no. But as the saying goes, "you screw what you gotta screw." A simple algebra equation should help you understand why men risk life, limb, and the wrath of special prosecutors to get laid.

Let's say A = the degree of sexual pleasure experienced from cheating, measured in hours spent skeeting (typically about 0.001). And let's say B = The shit you're going to take from your significant other, measured in hours she'll spend making your life a living hell (typically 5,000).

If A < B (e.g. 0.001 < 5,000), a dude generally won't bother.

But then there's the C factor—your degree of horniness, measured in how many hours you would spend waiting if a sorcerer told you, "Penelope Cruz is riding a horse this way and you'll definitely 100% get to nail her when she shows up naked, all you have to do is sit around for a while." When you multiply this in, the equation looks a little like this:

$$0.0004 \times \infty > 5,000$$

Of course, this is when a "reality jack" comes in handy. Take out the C factor and you suddenly have the power to say,

"Maybe this isn't worth it," at which point your cooler head will prevail. You may literally be saving your life, since screwicide also refers to situations in which (speaking of bareback riding) you're too horny to fetch a rubber while hooking up with a "pigskin"—a girl who's been passed around by the football team.

In this version of the equation, C equals the amount of hours you'll spend shedding manTears over the fact that you hooked up with a **herpitrator** and now have warts in your shorts for all of **herpituity**.

GUYKU #5
Homecoming next week . . .
Wonder if those blonde twins have
Matching STDs.
—JOHN WHEELER-RAPPE

Screwrette's – A condition that causes you to yell out inappropriate things while screwing.

We all say thoughtless, regrettable, even insane things during the heat of the moment. It's important to explain to your partner that you didn't actually mean it when you barked out "I love you"—you were actually suffering from a **screwrological disorder**.

skeet-n-greet – A hook-up where only after you do the chick do you find out who the hell she is. Sometimes when a girl introduces herself to you, you don't bother listening to any of the vagibberish that comes out of her mouth because you're pretty sober and you figure *no way in hell*. Many shots later, you've hooked up with someone whose name might as well be Rumpledsheepskin. Or maybe you spend the whole night talking about your mutual love of Jägermeister, only to wake up the next morning to discover it's not the only German thing she likes—she's got a collection of

Hitler dolls on her mantle and she's thanking you for having possibly given her a blue-eyed baby. *Hell-o!* Should you find yourself in such a quandary, feel free to hand the girl the following form to fill out:

Skeet-n-greet Questionnaire

Hi! You've just slept with me but I have no idea who you are. By answering a few simple questions you'll be providing me with information that I will probably ignore just like when you told it to me the first time, but this way I'll have it written down in case something pops up and I ever need to talk to you again.

Name (stripper name is fine): _____

Age (if under 18, please destroy this document): _____

Phone number (cell phone only, texting will do just fine): _____ - _____ - _____

Profession (only if it's something cool, otherwise I don't care): _____

If you answered "bartender/waitress" to the above, name of bar/restaurant where you can hook me and my friends up with free drinks/food: _____

If you answered "publicist," "customer service," etc., list any and all freebies that you can score me:
_____
_____
_____

Other assets (be specific as possible about location of vacation home you might let someone you're dating stay at, make/model of car you might let him drive, etc.):

_____

_____

_____

How hot are your female friends on a scale of 1 to 10: _____

Have they hooked up with guys you've dated in the past? Y / N (circle one)

Name of the one you could be talked into having a threesome with: _____

Stuff you can do in bed that we didn't already do (be specific):

_____

_____

_____

Last three guys you dated, with phone numbers. They will only be called if we end up dating and I start suspecting that you're a stripper:

_____

_____

_____

How insane would you say you are, with 1 being "I think I'm pretty sane" (i.e. you are a bit nuts) and 10 being "I'm a handful" (i.e. you're batshit): _____

What's your favorite color? _____

If you answered the above, what made you think I care?

_____

_____

_____

What would you rate me in bed, with 1 being awesome and 10 being totally awesome? _____

Do you have any STDs? Y / N (circle one)

If you answered no to the above, it's possible you do now. Sorry about that.

skeetotaler – A teetotaler in matters of skeeting: "You're not coming with us to the massage parlor? Don't be such a skeeto-taler."

spermission – Permission to release sperm. When you're barebacking, it's important to employ "spew diligence" and get the girl's **blow-ahead** before you blow your load. This is especially true when she's deepthroating you—you need to make sure she's ready to receive your **spewcharist**.

spewmiliate – To humiliate a girl by spewing on her in a foul and spracktacular way, for instance by creating "pop art" on her stomach. A girl is usually willing to "take one on the chin," and no harm in giving her a little "tits spritz." But it's important that you don't make a cockery out of her. Know your **jizcosity**—the viscosity and velocity of your jiz. If you think it's going to be a dribble but it turns out to be **Viagra falls**, you're likely to accidentally spunk in her hair and give her a "sperm perm." Avoid doing this or you'll catch some serious "sprack flak."

splaycation (also laycation) – When you get some rest, splay chicks, and get laid.

When men first started visiting other countries, they were shocked and appalled to see the natives running around without any clothes on. But these days the *only* reason to travel is to sit back and think to yourself, "The natives are getting dressless!" while two Hawaiian chicks prepare to lay you. Indeed there's nothing like combining T&A with R&R—and make no mistake, "relaxation" refers to "full relax" massages.

Whether you're traveling to TJ to get a BJ or visiting the former U.S.S.R. in search of P-U-S-S-Y, it's important to remember the old expression: "When in Rome, do who the Romans do." Don't worry—even if you don't know the language, you won't have trouble using **sexperanto** to turn a Thai girl into your personal, rumpshaking fly girl.

splaygiarism – Plagiarizing someone's sex moves, for instance a porn star's.

stallywacker – A tallywacker that's as big as a stallion's.

> GUYKU #6
> *I would consent to*
> *Lose an inch off my cock for*
> *A real lightsaber.*
> —TOM YOUNG

tailsafe – A failsafe or plan B that insures you'll get tail, sometimes called a **blueblocker** because she prevents you from getting blue balls, or a **ballternate**.

Let's say you suspect you're in for a blue-balling. Your date has only agreed to go out with you because you have Madonna tickets. You're pretty sure she isn't going to "put her hands all over your body." Enter the tailsafe. When your Doug Booty inevitably bounces in the end zone and Plan A blows you off instead of blowing you, you can immediately call your back-up plan—or, your back-that-ass-up plan. Of course it's only fair to let your tailsafe know you may be calling, though you shouldn't be so crass as to tell her exactly why. Earlier in the day, tell her something like, "I'm going to watch the game with the guys tonight—if my team wins, is it okay if I bring some champagne over to your place to celebrate?" Of course you'll show up without any Dom P, but you still might get some P.

Tampaxccident – An instance of accidentally having sex with a girl while her tampon is in, because she's too drunk to remember she's wearing it. When you do a girl, take great care to make sure you aren't being literally cock blocked by a **knobstacle**.

tapprehension – A girl's apprehension about having her booty tapped: "She was a little tapprehensive at first but when I told her I wasn't packing a weapon of ass destruction, she said, OK, go crazy. By the time I finished, I even gave her a **backdoorgasm**."

tête-à-tit – When you use a girl's boob as a **headbreast**.

the trim reaper – Anything that kills your chances at trim. Let's say you're working a girl and her boyfriend calls: You've just received a visit from the trim reaper. Let's say you're bagging a **wonder-age girl** who may or may not be legal and her parents burst in the room with the po-po: Blue-balled by the scythe of the trim reaper. Then there's Sam Cooke—wearing nothing but a shoe and an overcoat he chased a hooker who had fled his hotel room only to be shot by the hotel manager: A rare double visit from the grim reaper *and* the trim reaper.

trimspiration – When the prospect of getting trim inspires you to do something, whether it's losing weight, grooming yourself, or brushing up on your knowledge of French "Nouvelle Vague" movies.

trimtelligence – Intimate information about someone that only his or her sexual partner can possess.

When a woman caves to your foot-job fetish seemingly out of generosity, make no mistake she's getting something out of it too, and not just killer gludes: She's acquiring **trimtelligence**.

When trimtelligence works in your favor (say, an ex-fling has told one of her friends about your amazing **Lionel Richies**—the move where your fingers "dance on the ceiling"), it can get you laid before she's even laid eyes on you. But it can work against you, too: Interpol's bassist Carlos D. was the victim of a website called "Carlos D. Has Herpes."

Unfortunately, controlling the flow of trimtelligence is nearly impossible, since most chicks abide by the Freedom of Him-formation Act. If someone is spreading damaging trimtelligence about you, simply discredit the source. Saying she's a "crazy bitch" usually works. You can also get a second source to spread positive trimtelligence. If an ex posts a picture of your manpon on her MySpace page, get one of your female friends to leave a comment that she has seen your ween and it is actually much bigger.

Viagravated assault – When you're as horny as a Viagra popper and you twist your girl's arm till she finally agrees to do it with you.

whoremitory – The Fortress of Ballitude that you bring girls back to after you score with them (in polite company it can be called a **scoremitory**). It's your Whorea Bora, where you go caveman on girls.

whorensic evidence – Evidence of whorendous behavior that resembles something you'd find at a crime scene.

It's not unusual to wake up with no idea what or who you did last night and nothing but a few clues to help you out: A used Troj stuck to the wall, a single blonde hair on the pillow next to you, a gruesome blood spot in the middle of the bed. Gradually the pieces come together and you make a guess that it was Mrs. White in the dining room with a 12-inch dildo.

Whorensic evidence doesn't just help you figure out what sort of illicit cracktivities you engaged in the previous night—it also allows other girls to bust you. Sure, you can tell her those soiled panties she found in the hamper are *your* underwear, but "if they don't fit, she'll give you shit."

Taint any whorensic evidence that can and will be used against you. If you have a soiled panty, soil it further by using it as "panty Raid"—that's when you use her undergarment in lieu of bug spray, to squash the roaches in your apartment. After this, dispose of the panty immediately, otherwise its owner could somehow end up back at your apartment asking why there are dead insects in her undies—did you lend them to some skank with crabs? There's also the horrifying possibility that in a moment of forgetfulness you'll put on your **lace mask**—a panty face mask—and instead of breathing in sweet, sweet female goodness, roach bits will fly up your nose. You don't want this.

wintercourse – Intercourse that occurs in the winter, usually due to increased nesting impulses. Sometimes called "cold cocking."

When the temperature goes down, the women go down on you. The **whorecast** calls for brain. All you have to do is go on Craigslist to find a "snowblower" who'll make it a December to remember. By the end of the month you'll have gotten tons of gifts from Panty Claus—the Jolly Ol' St. Dick who brings you hos, hos, hos.

wrinkle cream – An instance of creaming in the company of an older woman: "Dude, I really applied the wrinkle cream the other night—I went home with this woman who must've been over sixty. She wasn't a cougar, man, she was a **ginasaur**." Just remember, there's no shame in 69ing a woman who's 69— sometimes you have to call up the oldest trick in your book and give her a little Bedicare. Even if she's as old as Madeleine Albright, she might just keep the bed rattling all night.

Xavier Roberts – A signature that indicates you've given a woman a child, much like the signature that's on the butt of every Cabbage Patch Kid: "This girl is the One, man. I'm going to put my Xavier Roberts on her baby's ass."

5

HOCABULARY

(n.) Vocabulary that applies to the often maddening behavior of hos

Women aren't just "playmates," there to serve you in bunny ears and have their asses slapped while Jack Nicholson shares his golf secrets with you. They can do everything men can do and even some stuff men *can't* do, like giving birth—and making you wish you had never been born. For a guy to make you regret the moment you were conceived, he'd have to make like Jean-Claude Van Damme and thoroughly pummel you with roundhouse kicks to the jaw. But a girl can do it just by saying, "I'm staying at my sister's house tonight. Don't call me."

To talk about chicks, you need more than just **banguage**. That's why words like "nag" were invented. For hundreds of years a "nag" referred to an old riding horse. In the 1800s the shotgun was invented. When a woman got on her husband's nerves he would go out to the backyard and shoot a horse, just to calm himself down. Soon there weren't a lot of nags left, and by the mid-1800s the meaning of the word was transferred to describe a woman who makes you want to blow a horse's brains out. (The origin of the word "deadhorse" is another thing entirely . . .)

Of course "nagging" is a very broad term. Even if you repeat it three times—*"nag nag nag"*—it still doesn't quite describe what your girl has done to become a total catheter. More specific words are needed. When she nags you because you haven't seen her in the past couple of days, you might say she's applying **see-her pressure.** This is one of the very worst forms of peer pressure, and yet there aren't any PSAs about it. You'll never see a TV ad that says, "It's 4 a.m., do you know where your balls are?" or "These are your balls. This is your wife on your balls." Crack! Sizzle!

With that in mind, here are a handful of words that will help you wax women—as in, talk about them, not *literally* wax them. Although that would be hot.

astrolobitch – A girl who uses astrology in a bitchy manner.

Girls think dudes are petty because they won't talk to a girl who's "sans cans," but chicks shut guys down for a way more shallow reason—because of their birth month. How many times have you been **astrolodissed**? Rejected **starbitrarily** just because you were born under a bad sign? Tell a chick you have cancer and she'll at least give you a sympathy lay before saying she doesn't want to get too attached, but tell her you *are* a Cancer and she'll say, "We'll never work out. Cancers are deceptive and manipulative." Ouch! Should've just stuck to lying to her that you have cancer.

Don't let one of these psychic psychos get you **astrolopissed**—getting into a **stargument** will only feed her conviction that Leos are hot-headed. Instead, cut these self-appointed **starbiters** off at the pass when they ask for your birthdate. Make up a story about why you don't like to tell people when you were born—maybe something about your mom dying during childbirth. She'll say, "Wow that's intense—I can tell you're a Scorpio", but as long as you neither confirm nor deny, you're probably safe from her lunar-cycle lunacy.

Finally, be wary of astrolobitches who exploit their own star signs, especially **whorpios** who use the fact that they were born between October 24 and November 22 as an excuse to hook up with all of your friends.

bag hag – 1. A woman who only dates douchebags and seeks them out at wanker-banker bars and other **douchetinations**. These girls believe that a kiss can magically transform a chode into a prince. 2. A woman who covets tacky bags.

Certain Carrie Bagshaws think that just by toting a Marc Jackoff bag they can assume the **hophistication** of Carrie Bradshaw—Sarah Jessica Parker's vagigantically annoying character in *Sex and the City*. Little do they know that what they see as a sexy quilted bag with a cute little clasp and stylish golden chain, we see as a barf bag. Even when a girl is attached to her bag like a colostomy patient, it isn't hard to get it away from her so you can puke into it. Girls love making guys their **purse nurse** by asking you to carry their Louis V. for them when they have to hoist something heavy like a Hello Kitty umbrella. Ironically they consider you a consummate gentleman if you're willing to stand around with their bag—clearly the *only* bag you need.

ballbatross – A controlling girlfriend that is constantly on your balls.

blobfuscate – To attempt to obfuscate one's fat, usually by wearing excessively revealing or concealing outfits, or painfully ugly **ouchfits**.

It's pretty flabbergasting, but girls who put on a lot of weight are often the ones who *don't* put on a lot of clothes. It's like they don't understand that you should only wear a revealing outfit when you can "pull it off"—or rather, make *men* want to pull it off. A girl with a lot of **cellublight** shouldn't traipse around in an itsy bitsy bikini—that's **fatrocious**. Better to create a **blobtical illusion** by wearing something black and slimming.

Chicks on social networking sites will often try to blobfuscate their double chins by tilting their heads at certain angles, or they'll take their profile photos from above. The most popular way to blobfuscate, of course, is to accentuate the breasts. A girl may have low self-esteem but high **shelf esteem**. In fact she might even be a **cleavangelist**, a woman who preaches about her boobs to anyone who'll listen. For better or worse, the only way to get a **knocker talker** to shut up about her giant jigglers is to get her to stick them in her mouth.

brantourage – A bevy of scantily clad female followers, sometimes referred to as a "stable of bitches."

Hopefully, there comes a time in every player's life when he has more chicks than he can shake a dick at. It's an "embarrassment of bitches." Keeping them away from each other no longer becomes viable—you can't take a new date to a bar or a restaurant, because you're dating waitresses and bartenders at every single place in town. At a certain point, you're going to have to consolidate these women into one big happy family, sort of like Manson's children. A brantourage is slightly different than a harem—think "Flavor of Love," not "Big Love."

So how do you get a bunch of girls who are getting it on with you to get along with each other? Consider yourself a conductor trying to cultivate a **whorechestra**. Chicks don't like chicks that remind them of themselves or even chicks that are wearing their same outfit, so instead of two oboes, pick an oboe and a clarinet. Your skin flute will thank you for it.

Here are a few instruments that can easily mess up your mix, and some advice on how to wave your baton at them:

THE ALPHA CHICK

Defining trait: A nipply narcissist who insists on attention at all times.

Coping mechanism: Leave this one alone—she's bad for your bone.

Bangability: Strictly bag and release.

THE NYMPHO

Defining trait: Tongues your ear and pretty much dry-humps you while you're trying to work other members of your brantourage.

Coping mechanism: Don't alienate her by pushing her away. Whenever she jumps you, be polite but maintain a stiff posture and a grimace to make it clear to the other members of your brantourage that you wouldn't touch this skank with your ten-inch pole.

Bangability: When a girl is on you like an STD, resisting her is out of the question. Do everything with her that allows you to still say truthfully, "I have never had sexual relations with that woman."

THE BRAINY BRAIN DONOR

Defining trait: Doesn't understand why you hang out with these bimbos. Likes Emily Dickinson more than she likes dick.

Coping mechanism: To bring her into the fold, make it clear that you need her around to save you from these idiots. Exchange secret grins anytime one of them says something imbecilic and make her think you will one day cast them off.

Bangability: Bang away. Her journal will be the only one to know.

THE CHICK LOVER

Defining trait: Would rather hang with the girls than see how hung you are. "I looooove your friends," Chick Lover squeals, and then does her best to commandeer them, suggesting shopping trips and chick flicks.

Coping mechanism: While the chick lover can be the glue that holds your brantourage together by making them feel more like a group of friends than a pack of groupies, she can also steal them from you. Limit her time with the brantourage while simultaneously using her as bait. When members of your brantourage inevitably start asking, "I don't know, is [Chick Lover] going?" say, "I don't know—I bet she will if you do" whether you've invited her or not.

Bangability: Do her early in the game, before she really becomes friends with everyone. Otherwise, she may use post-coital awkwardness as an excuse to cut out the middleman and steel your stable.

THE FAG HAG

Defining trait: Only hangs out with you and all these other women because she thinks you're gay.

Coping mechanism: The fag hag bolsters your brantourage by making you seem less threatening and by adding a bit of intrigue. Your sexuality becomes a mystery that needs to be solved. But be careful that the Fag Hag doesn't share her theories with a Chatty Cathy that you've actually bagged, or you'll be outed big time.

Bangability: Tell her you've never done it with a woman before in order to get her into the sack—then kick her out of the brantourage before she can blab about it.

THE FATTY

Defining trait: Obesity, low self-esteem.

Coping mechanism: Fatties are totally unthreatening to other chicks.

Bangability: Have at it. Even if the others find out they'll either refuse to believe it, feel sorry for you, or be impressed by your lack of judgmentalism. Be careful, however, not to let the fatty see you working skinnier chicks after you've hooked up with her. In a brantourage, a resentful fatty is dead weight.

breastpionage – The act or practice of spying on a chick's breasts. It's your duddy duty to seize any and all **gawkertunities**, no matter where you are, who you're with, or who your target is with. Is she leaning over a wheelchair to adjust her ailing grandmother's

IV tube? Bust out the **skinoculors**. Is she wearing "pas de bra" while pooper scooping? Put on your **guyfocals**. It's important to have good "scoping mechanisms," or you'll never be able to properly **cleavaluate** a woman. You're going to encounter plenty of **gawkward** situations where you're not sure whether or not you should satisfy your **chimpulses**, but in the end those basic animal needs must be met. When flesh is being flashed, peeping is **oglebligatory**.

It can't be said enough: No self-respecting "Two-can Sam" misses a copportunity—a chance to cop a glance. Even if you're too short to peep from above, you can become "Pair Jordan" and leap three feet off the ground to get a new pervspective. Or simply wait for a woman in a loose dress to bend over and reveal everything from "cleave to beav." Who cares if you develop a reputation as Sir Glancealot?

Whatever you do, don't become a **titiot**—someone who's totally "nipple crippled." Go into "breast arrest" and you'll find yourself **booby babbling**, inserting Freudian slips into conversations with co-workers: "It's great to have you here, Carol. Breast of luck!" Or: "Great job on that account, Sharon. You really nippled that one right in the bud. I mean, nipped that right in the boob. I mean . . ."

Yes, even the most eagle-eyed of "rack hawks" get "busted"— and just like that it's **rack hawk down**. Before you get flack for checking out a chick's rack, immediately compliment her blouse or necklace (which explains why you were looking in that area) and ask what it's made of (which quickly changes the subject). You might even say "Where can I get one of those for my girlfriend?" (*"one* of those," not "those"). If she actually calls you out, just tell her she's being **pairanoid**. Or tell her, "To stare is human. To forgive is divine."

While trying to take advantage of **peepertunities**, you're always going to face **gawk blockers**. If some guy steps in to ask you why you're checking out his wife, tell him you have no idea what he's talking about (don't take your hand out of your pocket or he might see your chub). If the girl is blonde, for instance, say, "No offense but she's not my type—I like Asians." Of course, if the dude is a lot smaller than you, just say, "Fuck you and the whore you rode in on!"

> GUYKU #7
> *A woman's bosom*
> *Um uhh, er . . . um . . . huh? . . . um . . . wait . . .*
> *What was I saying?*
> —JASON WISHNOW

broing along – Going along with the bros.

Nothing beats a girl who's willing to "play with your boys"—in *both* senses! But be careful, as time goes by, your bros might start thinking of her as Broko Ono—a girlfriend who seems cool at first but ends up insidiously trying to break up your band of brothers. This can really mess with your head—*Is she giving me this stand-up Guitar Hero machine because she's the one girl cool enough to let me play it in the apartment 24/7, or is it because she's trying to make me spend less time playing it with my bros at Futtbuckers?* Don't let it get to you! Remember that your boys have their own brotivations when they accuse her of ruining the guynamic—after all, you're the one with the unlimited Futtbuckers gaming card. Without you they're lost.

cashstrate – To castrate by having way more cash than you: "The dinner tab bounced my credit card and she whipped out two Benjis. She totally cashstrated me."

chargument – An argument that leads to a house or drinking establishment burning down—for instance when Left Eye Lopes burned her man's mansion to the ground.

crampage – A rampage brought on by PMS cramps. "Yo, let's get some brews tonight. I need to get out of the house because my girl's on a crampage."

dresspionage – Trying to peep up a girl's dress.

Practicing dresspionage is nowhere near as easy as breastpionage: Unless they're Paris or Britney getting out of a car, women practice **cuntcealment** with much greater care than they do **mammouflage**. By middle school, girls know to cross their legs when sitting down in front of you, and you'd have to be Moses himself to will a parting of the knees. It's a mind freak that couldn't even be accomplished by the greatest sexual magician of them all, David Cop-a-feel. Usually the best you can hope for is Visible Panty Line or a whale tail (thong strings emerging from a woman's pants), but now and then you'll get a classic upskirt and find yourself in the land of silk and honey, or if she *isn't* wearing panties, you might even get a full-on gash flash. To that end, remain in a state of constant skirt alert, keeping your eyes peeled for the labia at the end of the tunnel.

dumpedfounded – Dumbfounded as to why you were dumped.

Just because you blow money on a girl doesn't mean she'll blow you—she may well end up blowing you off. Still, certain players are so "cocksure" that they refuse to accept the possibility that at the end of the night they'll get the cold shoulder instead of a rusty trombone. When she declines to go on another date, they tell her, "Come on, please? You haven't even gone for a ride in my Lexus!" This sort of **douchebegging** is simply unacceptable. And don't ask stupid questions like, "Was it someone I did?" Getting dumped is *not* an opportunity for introspection and self-improvement—chicks are the ones who stay home downing bonbons. *You* need to go out and grope tatas. Sure it sucks to be smitten with a girl only to get smited by her, but as the saying goes—when you get thrown, climb right back on the whores.

duty text – To text your girlfriend out of obligation, not because you actually want to communicate with her or to booty text her. "Watch my beer, guys—I gotta duty text my girlfriend."

emascudate – To date a man in such a way as to emasculate him.

What's the first thing you do after convincing an admissions board that you're worthy of their college? You move in, put up a *Jackass* poster, and fire up the bong. Dating is the same way—girls know that if they "give it up" they can also give up all hope that you'll ever be a gentleman again. That's why they sometimes **bluemiliate** you, blueballing you over the course of several dates so that you'll continue to go to geometric dance recitals with them. Fair enough—you'll get your nads back when you ball her.

Some girls, however, insanely expect you to do this stuff *after you've started hooking up.* She might want you to be her "purse nurse." Maybe she sends you on **whore chores** all the time. Or she gives your tallywacker a horrifying **prudeonym** like "Mr. Sprinkles." When you're being emascudated, consult your bros to see whether she deserves a "piece-of-ass pass." It's easier to be your girl's bitch if she's so hot she makes all your bros go, "You da man."

fembellishment – A distinctly female form of exaggeration.

Chicks are well aware that if they told their friends how you actually treat them, they'd raise a manicured pointer finger, purse their lips, make their head do that "I don't think so" thing, and say, "*Girlfriend, you better kick him to the curb.*" That's why they learn to see male behavior in the most positive light possible. When you take her to Denny's and do her out back by the dumpster, she'll swoon, "He took me to a nice restaurant and made love to me under the stars." After just a few dates she's telling everyone you're her "boyfriend" and soon the fifty-cent laser-pointer ring you got out of a vending machine and only gave to her because it sucked becomes a "promise ring."

Watch out for these common "miss interpretations":

COLD, HARD REALITY	FEMBELLISHMENT
You bring her to the bar where your bros are watching the game so you can go on a "date" without having to hear her yap all night.	"He already introduced me to all of his friends. I think his family is next."
You open a cab door for her so that while she's getting in you can sneak one last peek at the club's smoking-hot doorwoman.	"He's such a gentleman, always opening doors for me..."

COLD, HARD REALITY	FEMBELLISHMENT
You smack her ass because it looks hot in that "squirt skirt."	"He's so loving—he's not afraid to show affection in public."
She agrees to an act of screwmiliation and you say, "See, this is what I love about you!"	"He told me he's in love with me."
You tell her you believe in open relationships.	"He said he was open to a relationship."
You do anal with her so you can cross one last thing off the list before you tell her it's not going to work out.	"He asked me to share a very special part of myself with him. He must want to be with me forever."
You dump her.	"I broke up with him. He turned out to be a jerk."

femcroachment – When a chick encroaches on your personal space or your established routine.

When guys say they "need space" they sometimes mean it quite literally—suddenly you don't have anywhere to shave because your sink is cluttered with her curling iron, her makeup, and her manic depression meds. To avoid becoming the victim of a "hostile makeover," you must first identify areas in your home that might be compromised.

TARGET AREA	ITEMS IT'S *OKAY* FOR HER TO LEAVE	OFFENDING ITEMS, AND YOUR EXCUSE FOR THROWING THEM AWAY
The coffee table	A note with a number that says "Call me."	Issues of *Cosmo, Glamour*, etc.: "Sorry, I figured they were available online."
The fridge	Beer.	Tofu, prune juice, carrots, etc.: "It looked like they were going bad. Yes, even after two days. Do I look like I know anything about tofu?"

TARGET AREA	ITEMS IT'S OKAY FOR HER TO LEAVE	OFFENDING ITEMS, AND YOUR EXCUSE FOR THROWING THEM AWAY
The bathroom	Toilet paper, since you've probably gone a week without it.	Feminine hygiene products: "I got high the other night and made a log cabin out of tampons, using your toothpaste to simulate snow on the roof. Unfortunately I put a candle in the middle and the whole thing burned down. Those things are highly flammable! In fact I'm not sure I'm comfortable having them around the house..."
Your computer	Her e-mail open, so you can read her friend's message, "What do you think of my new Brazilian (photo attached)?"	Two-hundred-page term paper she'll need to come back and work on: "My computer said it had a virus. You mean you didn't back it up?"
Your bedroom	Holaroids you took of her the night before.	Items of clothing: "I took them to get washed and the guys at the laundry lost it all. Don't worry, I'm suing them. The court case could take months, perhaps years."

It's one thing when femcroachment is limited to your dwelling, but what happens when your girl starts breaking down formerly sacred personal boundaries with all of the fervor of an East German sledgehammering her way into the West? Do you just sit around and listen to the winds of change? How do you politely make her realize that you don't want her to join in your reindeer games?

ACTIVITY SHE WANTS TO BUTT IN ON	WHY YOU AREN'T HAVING IT	YOUR EXCUSE
Watching the game	She'll be like an annoying two-year-old, asking, "Daddy, what's a touchdown? What's a fumble? What's a pigskin?"	You're superstitious—for twenty years you haven't let anyone whose first name starts with [her initial] watch the game with you because it jinxes your team. This includes your mom. "Sorry babe, I know it's crazy but that's just the way it is. When my team wins I'll buy you a milkshake."
A strip trip	No matter how cool she pretends to be with it, she'll hold it against you that you'd cupgrade to a stripper faster than you can spell Enchanté.	"The guys there are pigs and you're so beautiful—would you want me to get into a horrible fight when they molest you and harass you?"
A family vacation	Your mom will grow attached to her, making it impossible to dump her without being called a failure and being told for the rest of your life, "Why didn't you stay with that one girl..."	You're concerned about your "special" half-brother who always threatens to kill himself if he isn't allowed to dry-hump visitors and throw feces at them.
A friend or relative's wedding	She'll ruin your chances of hooking up with horny bridesmaids.	"It's really obnoxious—they're charging guests five hundred dollars per seat. I can't ask you to pay that." If she insists on paying that, tell her sorry, you promised to take a friend who needs to do research for her wedding. "She wants it to be perfect. You know how girls are."

ACTIVITY SHE WANTS TO BUTT IN ON	WHY YOU AREN'T HAVING IT	YOUR EXCUSE
Boys' night out	It's boys' night out.	"It's boys' night out. Deal or peel."
A drinks date with a hot female friend	She'll ruin your chances of hooking up with the friend.	Wait a minute, maybe she *should* come out. Threesome!

femtrapment – An instance of being asked a question that no woman should be allowed to ask, and that you'll definitely get busted on if you answer honestly.

It all started when Eve asked Adam, "Does this leaf make me look fat?" Adam responded, "Didn't the Big Dude tell us we were supposed to go around naked? I'm not sure that's a good idea," causing Eve to go apeshit on him: "You think I'm fat, don't you?" Luckily Adam didn't have to deal with this much longer because God immediately evicted both of their asses.

This sort of **fataclysm** isn't the only instance of fem-trapment.

HER QUESTION	ANSWER YOU KNOW IS WRONG	ANSWER YOU THINK MIGHT BE RIGHT	ACTUAL CORRECT ANSWER
"Do you love me as much as when we first met?"	"It's funny, I was just talking about this with the new girl I've started dating..."	"Love is not linear—it's like a tide that flows and ebbs. Except that while marine biologists can track such things, love is immeasurable."	"Yes, of course I love you as much as when we first met."

HER QUESTION	ANSWER YOU KNOW IS WRONG	ANSWER YOU THINK MIGHT BE RIGHT	ACTUAL CORRECT ANSWER
"Do you think my sister/mom/friend is prettier than me?"	"You mean in real life or in my fantasies where she is naked but for a broadsword?"	"I don't think in terms of one thing being more beautiful than another—is one brushstroke of a painting more beautiful than another? It's all part of this beautiful thing called life."	"No, of course I don't think your sister/mom/friend is prettier than you."
"Would you ever hook up with [name of one of your or her female friends]?"	"You mean, again?"	"I've learned that even when you're talking about the most farfetched situations, you can never say never. I never thought I would end up with you and now here we are! Together!"	"No, of course I wouldn't hook up with [name of friend]."
"Have you ever paid for sex?"	"Never in actual dollars. Just foreign currencies."	"That's an interesting question—doesn't one 'pay for sex' on a first date? And isn't money just a meaningless social construction anyway?"	"No, of course I've never paid for sex."
"Do I look fat?"	"You mean, compared to someone who *doesn't* look fat?"	"Our society puts undue pressure on women to be unnaturally skinny—in other cultures women your size are considered 'healthy' and 'robust.' "	"No, of course you don't look fat."

Be aware that girls often send their friends on **heconnoissance missions**, to ask stuff like, "So are you serious about this relationship?" or "How do you feel about her?" It's **friendtrapment**. There's no way to answer correctly, especially since the friend is sure to completely **fembellish** everything you say anyway. Simply answer with something vague and quickly change the subject: "I like her a lot. I mean . . . you know her! How long *have* you known her?" As she babbles on about their entire history since pre-school, motion to *your* friends for help.

Flack Friday – An expression that indicates the inevitability of getting flack from your boys on Friday because you need to hang out with your girl or flack from your girl because you're with your boys.

Your girlfriend knows that you can't spell weekend without the "we"—float the idea that "Friday is guy day" and it'll fly about as well as the Hindenburg. In her mind Friday is "*my* day," and there's no convincing her otherwise, especially if she's a "weekend worrier" who spends the entire week fretting about what she and you are going to do the second Friday rolls around. This is a total catheter since movies are released on Fridays meaning you have to choose between seeing *Die Hard 20: Hard-On for Dying* with the guys or seeing *Thirty, Purdy, and Flirty* with your girl.

It's a classic **funundrum**—you're damned if you dude, damned if you don't. The benefit of choosing the chick flick over the dick flick is that next time she says "You never do anything I want to do," you can say, "But I saw that French movie about the hearing-impaired rapist with you six weeks ago." She'll point out that you spent the entire first part of the movie texting galibis ("sorry, cant hang 2nite—pounding this hot piece of a$$") and that you were eventually asked to leave the theater for snoring, but who can blame you? Like you're going to watch a movie with subtitles that's not a bukkake flick?

gaysay – To gainsay (i.e. deny or dispute) by saying, "He's gay!"

You get a 4 a.m. text that says, "Just saw your girl humping on some dude at Futtbuckers. Sorry bro." When your girl staggers through the door and you confront her she says, "Relax, James is gay! We were dancing to Madonna!" You ask her why there's a spewvenir on her collar and she says, "Oh, that's nothing! James jacked his boyfriend off and it accidentally landed on me. Gay clubs are crazy! Everyone was just having fun." Later, you ask her why the words "I did your girlfriend doggie-style and loved every second of it" are written in Sharpie on her back and she says, "Oh, James did me from behind, but it's fine, he's gay. That's just his sense of humor."

Girls use the GBF (Gay Best Friend) excuse because outing someone is an easy out. If you find a bar napkin with some dude's digits on it, she knows she can avoid hours of arguing by saying, "Oh, my girlfriend gave me the number of her gay best friend— I'm going to set him up with *my* gay best friend. Gaygaygaygaygay."

Usually you never actually get to meet these guys, since that would mean having to go to a poetry reading at Pink Pages or leather night at the Bottom Feeder—*or so she says*. Even when you do get to manalyze them, it's hard to tell whether they're truly pink or whether it's all a rougey ruse. Just because he starts pawing at your girlfriend's tits in front of you doesn't mean he's straight. He might just be a **douchefag**—the sort of gay guy who acts like a total douche because he's totally **boobsessed**. To find out what's what, offer to set him up with one of your bros and see if he goes for it. If he *does*, you're going to owe that bro of yours—*big time*.

ginaralize – To generalize about vaginas.

Guys love to make "blanket generalizations" about how certain types of chicks are under the covers. Even a nookie rookie who's only done it once in his life—with a pimply albino pygmy—will insist that pimply albino pygmies give the best head and will construct an elaborate theory to prove it.

In addition to ginaralizing about which race, religion, bra size, or hair color is most whack in the sack, dudes also make ginaralizations about how to get them there: Perhaps you hold a theory that Asian chicks love to flirt, but the second you try to seal the deal they give you the "Great Wall of China."

It's important to confine ginaralizations to barticulation. They're generally frowned upon when professed in public, as was the case in 2006 when Governor Arnold Schwarzenegger said Latin chicks were hot tempered. (Seriously though, it's totally true. I hooked up with this Puerto Rican chick once who . . .)

guyjack – When a guy highjacks a girl from the dude she's with, also called "ho poaching."

Taking a hot chick into a testosterzone is as bold as wearing a twenty-four-karat chain in the ghetto. When she's the one person at the hockey game wearing a tube top and hot pants, she's a veritable "diamond in the buff," and you can bet everyone around you is going to want to snag your piece of snatch. Stadium seating makes for great pervspective, meaning the dudes in the rows above you will be keeping their eye on her paps instead of the puck. Don't leave your seat, no matter how much you want those super nachos, or when you get back you might find that someone has escorted her up to his luxury skybox to be initiated into the Mile-High Stadium Club.

herrands (aka whore chores) – Emasculating errands that you're forced to run for your girlfriend. The only time it's acceptable to run an errand for a girl is if you're helping her do something for you—for instance if she's asking you to go out and buy some KY for an act of screwmiliation, and *maybe* to score some ingredients while she's cooking for you. But run the other way if she's the type to pitch a fit because you came back from her health food store with tempeh instead of tofu. Nobody likes a "tempeh tantrum."

ho-bot – A chick who's hot but has the personality of an automaton; also called a **hot-tomaton**.

Certain smoking-hot chicks have all the intelligence of

smoking-*pot* chicks—they consider the brain an accessory just like their heart-shaped ankle locket or their Juicy Couture bag. In fact if they literally had half a frontal lobe and the other half was on sale at Bloomingdale's, they'd only buy it because it's pink. Of course, it's not like you want a first date to tell you about her favorite existential philosophers—that would be pretty stupid. But a basic requirement is that she crack up at your hilarious jokes. If instead she just sits there and says, "That's funny," then you're probably in the company of a ho-bot.

ho couture – Clothing worn by a woman of loose morals and tight outfits.

If certain outfits "leave nothing to the imagination," why do you imagine yourself doing dirty things to the chicks who wear them? Some girls seem to do all of their shopping at the Salivation Army, picking out panties that leave us panting, tops that cause us to topple over, and bottoms imported from Sodom. They torture us by wearing what amounts to S&M gear. They make no attempt to hide their Victoria's Secret. Even in the workplace they wear tight-fitting, low-cut numbers that cause us to wonder what they look like in their double-breasted birthday suits. Here are some other items in a woman's **whoredrobe**:

bratas – When a flatchested chick uses a padded bra to simulate tatas.

"cup" caking – When a girl wears a bra that's too small for her, causing her boobs to spill over the rim.

easy-insert skirt – A skirt that's so small you could insert yourself into her without even lifting it up; also called a **squirt skirt**.

fannyhose – Leggings that are as tight as pantyhose and make her ass look banging.

flauntgerie – When a woman puts lace in your face by wearing visible lingerie.

hot pair balloon – A tube top that contains a hot pair in such a way that you could pop it with a pin and cause her tits to spill out.

little crack dress – A dress that fits snugly enough to show just a hint of buttcrack.

mascary – A scary amount of mascara.

name chain – A gold chain that spells her name in cursive, also spells trouble.

pit purse – A handbag that rests immediately below the armpit. Chicks usually wear these while they dance to cheesy-ass top-forty songs during Girls' Night Out. The closer to her armpit her purse is, the easier the chick is: If traces of deodorant can actually be found on the clasp she is a ho fo sho.

see-shirt – A tight T-shirt that's extremely **cleavealing**.

striplettos – Stilettos that only a stripper would wear.

tank pop – When breasts are practically popping out of a tank top.

tipstick – Lipstick that seems destined to end up on the tip of a penis.

whorts – Whorishly short shorts, usually with the word JUICY on the butt. Sometimes called **got 'em bottoms** since they show she has cheeks for weeks.

All of these whoredrobe items can and should be taken off, but there's nothing you can do about a **craptoo**. A Billy Bob Thornton tattoo isn't going to keep you from banging Angelina Jolie, but when it comes to your average chick, some body art is so **tattrocious** that it makes your pecker shrivel up like someone's coming at it with an electric needle. It's like these chicks were high as a kite went they looked through the **tatalogue**—the big catalogue of tat designs. Some examples of tats that'll make you think twice:

1. **A tit tat or a 'ttocktoo.** Is that a butterfly or a triple nipple?
2. **Anything with a face.** The last thing you want to look at when you're doing her from behind is a fatass Buddha.
3. **Asian typography or a tribal symbol on the lower back.** These tats basically say, "I felt like putting something on my body but I didn't care what." Chances are, she's just as careless about what or who she puts *in* her body.
4. **Her ex's name.** Inevitably it's going to make you wonder how hung the dude was and if it took *him* a half hour to get her off.
5. **A cracktoo.** Beware the chick who has "Abandon hope all ye who enter here" over her vadge or butt.
6. **A slutterfly.** A butterfly spreading its wings is a sure sign that she'll spread her legs.

ho-stalgia – Nostalgia for someone you've dated or banged.
Now and then it's fine to pound it to Holaroids of your ex, but get sucked into serious hostalgia and you might find yourself **tear jerking**—jerking off while weeping about the buns that got away. If you're experiencing hostalgia, it's best to just say "thank you for the mammaries" and leave it at that. Avoid the temptation to give yourself a "pics fix." Perform a full **ho-botomy** by deleting the girl's number from your phone—that way when you scroll through

your address book looking for chicks to booty text, she won't be a pussibility. If you can find a girl who looks like her, doppelbang her and then dump her. And of course don't go to places where you might run into her. A strip club is a pretty good bet for avoiding an ex. Unless she's a stripper—in which case go to a whorehouse.

> GUYKU #10
> *Horticulturists*
> *love plants. That must make me a*
> *planticulturist.*
> —CHRIS COOK

hot dog – A girl that, like a hot dog, is an amalgam of the lesser parts of hot girls. She's not as juicy as a grade-A steak but she'll hit the spot when you're really hungry.

jersey girl – A girl whose love of the game amounts to wearing the jersey of the player she thinks is hot. Can also be used to rag on a dude who wears the jersey of a pretty-boy atlethe.

Certain chicks try to achieve **fandrogyny** by wearing jerseys, caps, and the whole nine yards, but it's obvious their war paint is just another excuse to wear makeup. They'll tell you they like certain quarterbacks because of their glorious passes, when really it's all about their glorious asses. In fact they'd much rather see the QB make a pass at *them* than to the wide receiver.

Unlike dudes who have a fraudulent love of sports, jersey girls are fairly harmless as long as they know to dress in baby tees supporting their team rather than big, formless mammouflaging jerseys (why not buy them said baby tees for Chistmas, a size too small?). Though their bags tend to femcroach on your space when you're watching the game at the bar, they can actually make it more tolerable, since taking deep cleansing whiffs of their shampooed hair while you're behind them in line does much to subdue the unholy stench of piss, sweat, spilled beer, and puke all around you. That said, it's pointless to try to talk stats with them, so just ignore them in favor of engaging in **fandiloquence** with your bros, then give them an extra long, tight hug and slap on the ass when someone hits a homer.

jizdemeanor – An instance of jizzing that you consider a misdemeanor rather than a deeply criminal case of cheating on your girlfriend: "I don't get why she's flipping out because I got a happy ending from some mamasan—it's just a jizdemeanor."

legsibitionist – A girl who has legs and knows how to use them.

Sometimes you ask a guy if he's a knocks man or a 'ttocks man and he says, "I am the leg man, koo koo koo choo." Even if you're not a Thighsenhower, you probably experience some degree of **legscitement** when you see a leggy Peggy—if nothing else it's a nice contrast to midget porn. **Legstroverts** will often accentuate their gams by wearing Daisy Dukes and **spillettos**—stilettos she's likely to take a spill in before the night is over. Picking up one of these **gamazons** is no harder than complimenting her shoes—just make sure none of your bros are listening when you ask, "Are those Manolos?"

Little Ho Peep – A girl who, like Little Bo Peep separated from her sheep, has peeled off from her friends or boyfriend and is walking around dressed like a ho.

It happens every night—a girl dons her finest ho couture to eat out with her man. Halfway through the date the guy tells the waitress he wants to eat *her* out and the girl storms out in tears. She's wined up on Pinot Grigio and she has no idea where she is since he's the one who drove her to the restaurant. Plus she didn't bring a coat because she didn't expect to be out in the cold. Suddenly she's a Punxsutawney Jill—just another lost angel in the city of light.

It's your duty to get a Little Ho Peep away from the hordes of **vulvtures**. Make sure she gets home safe—preferably to *your* home safe! Politely ask her if she knows where she is, and resist the impulse to say, "You're in the jungle baby!!" If she seems disoriented, offer to escort her to a safe place such as the nearest Futtbuckers. Calm her down with a tall glass of firewater— hopefully she'll be so appreciative that you let her pour her heart out, she'll let you whip your dick out.

mace face – A face that makes you wish you were temporarily blind.

mammouflage – Camouflage of the mammary area that makes it hard to **breastimate**.

marrogance – The arrogance of a newly married man.

Everyone has at least one recently married friend who is convinced he has unlocked the secret of happiness. He's totally **snatchtached**, and brags about his in-house punani like he's the only dude who has ever walked into a Zales store and ignored the thought that installment payments on diamonds are forever. He tells you that one day you'll "grow out of" bachelorhood too, and hopes you meet someone as cool as his wife. You'd punch this **one chick pony** in the face but if he slugged you back, his wedding band would leave a mark. When this happens, simply one-up your bro by bringing hot fucks to his wife's potlucks. This makes it clear to him that you're a **playboy** while he's a **stayboy**—someone who's like a trained dog when it comes to answering to his bitch.

Martha Screwert – A girl who is anal in the bedroom—and not in the good way.

No matter how civilized a girl is at dinner, you hope that under the covers she's a total **sheanderthal**. But if you walk into her bedroom and see teddy bears sitting on a Laura Ashley floral-print quilt, you are pretty much screwed—and not in the good way! Obviously you're dealing with someone who is a total prude in the nude, and has a deep **screwrosis**. Be prepared to hear things like, "You're not doing it right" and "Ew, you just got a drop of sweat on me. Gross." Martha Screwerts often have endless rules of bediquette—put these pajamas and this sleeping cap on; tuck yourself under the covers and snuggle with me for an hour before we do anything; don't poke me with that thing. It's enough to make your head explode. And not in the good way!

perversatile – Able to adopt whatever perversion is necessary for the situation.

Life is full of perplexing choices—Paper or plastic? Shiite or Sunni? Mary Kate or Ashley? But the most enduring one has been with us since the dawn of the breast man and the dawn of the ass man. Are you a boob for boobs or an ass about ass? Are you glued to the gluteals or are you obsessed with the chest? When someone tells you tits are the tits, do you say, "But—the butt"? Or do you believe the rump is for chumps and breasts are the best? Are you a boobermensch or a booty man? Are you a glude dude or a total pairhead? It's possible nature intended us to choose knocks over 'ttocks—after all, they have nipples on them, sort of like cherries on top. But at the end of the day, it doesn't pay to be picky. After all, when a girl is giving you head, all you can see is the top of hers—which is why your only rule should be "No bald chicks." A wise bro once said, "At keggers you can't be choosers."

planties – Panties that a girl plants in order to blow your chances should another girl come over your house.

After a girl leaves your love nest, you should make a clean sweep of the area to make sure she hasn't planted any IEDs (that's Improvised Explosive Devices, not IUDs—*those* are her problem). Should you forget to do this because you're suffering from a bangover, at least have some stock answers prepared when the person who *does* find them asks you why there's a sparkle-glitter toothbrush in the bathroom.

THE WEAPON	METHOD OF DIFFUSING THE WEAPON WHEN A GIRL ASKS ABOUT IT
The chopper gun	Tell her you bought a second toothbrush to clean your toilet with. Why's it pink? So you'll remember not to brush your teeth with it.
The compact weapon	Tell her you bought that Revlon compact because you needed a small mirror for trimming your pubes.
The lipstick of dynamite	"I got that so I could show you my *Shining* impression. Check this out—'Redrum! Redrum!'"
The Secret weapon	"Well, it *is* strong enough for a man..."
Tampaxidental death	Remember, you can always say your sister or your chick friend came over because they don't have cable and had to catch their fave show.
Planties	"Those are just some **pantiques** I found in the closet. I was using them as **panty Raid**—you know, to smush roaches with."
Emptying the hair clip	"Oh, how embarrassing—I sometimes use that hair clip as a nipple clamp when I wack off. What's the scrunchie doing here? Um, cock ring?"

PMScalate – To escalate due to PMS: "Sorry dude, I can't go out tonight. My girl's paranoia has totally PMScalated and she's convinced I'm cheating on her. But say hi to the girl I hooked up with last week."

Stay with a girl long enough and you'll develop PMSESP—Premenstrual Syndrome Extrasensory Perception, a condition that causes you to register the fact that she's about to become a Raggedy Ann even before she has reached the **flipping point**. When this happens, **PMScape** before she flips the bitch switch, or rest assured, *there will be blood.*

primprisonment – Being turned into a girl's "primp gimp" while she puts her makeup on.

Tell your girl you're heading across the street to Chuck's to catch the last quarter of the game and she'll say "Oh wait for me,

I just need a sec to get ready." All well and good until she spends half an hour in front of the mirror primping herself to look like Boobzo the Clown. You **primplore** her to hurry up but she's **primpervious**, ignoring your demands while she applies face paint with all the meticulousness of Vincent Van Ho. By the time you walk across the street, the game's over, your boys are fellabrating, and you have no idea what happened. It's useless to try to rush a girl out the door. For her, going off half-chalked is not an option. You have no choice but to wait till she finishes—don't complain or she'll put her nose deeper in the powder, like Scarface.

Punxsutawney Jill – As spring approaches, the first chick to wear revealing clothes after a spell of cold weather. Though her outfit is hot during the day, she's left shivering at night and gets more attention than a groundhog coming up to see its shadow. When you see a Punxsutawney Jill, offer her some **mansportation** in your heated vehicle.

responsenility – Being senile about your responsibilities—usually as pertains to your relationship. Those who suffer from responsenility often forget that, for instance, they were supposed to get their asses up early to take out the trash. Or they neglect to remember they were supposed to get their boo a birthday present instead of going to the ballgame. The only way to cure this condition is to get a female friend to remind you when your girlfriend's birthday is.

retargument – A retarded argument you have with your girlfriend.

Chicks love arguing about stupid shit. You come home sixteen minutes after you said you would and she gives you the "late stare"—the hate stare that says, "You just spent sixteen minutes orangubanging a monkey at the zoo, didn't you?" Or you emerge from the bathroom and she gives you the "bate stare"—the one that says, "You just wacked it to the photo of my sister that's on the toilet, didn't you?" Your first mistake is to ask her, "What?" She says, "Nothing" in a tone that says, "Everything about you," and then your second mistake is to again ask, "*What?*" At this point you're like a port inspector giving the all-clear to a fertilizer ship—you've given her license to unload a bunch of bullshit.

Just like there are stages to coping with grief, there are stages to coping with a chick who's *giving* you grief—the first stage is denial: *You can't possibly be starting something over this. Not when I just treated you to the second cheapest wine on the list.* The second stage is anger: *I just treated you to the second cheapest wine on the list. Get off my balls!* The third is bargaining: *Fine, if I go to your parents' house and don't leave after just an hour this time, will you shut up?* The fourth is depression: *Jesus, I'm dating a psycho.* And the fifth is acceptance: *So I'm dating a psycho. Whatever. I'm still getting laid.*

In between the anger and acceptance phases there's often **fighcking**—a combination of fighting and fucking that occurs when you go from locking horns to knocking boots, as famously happened in *Brokeback Mountain*. Fighcking is totally different from your classic hatefuck—as opposed to hating her but still wanting to fuck, you hate *fighting* with her and would rather fuck.

Before you can fighck away your problems, however, you're going to have to engage in the classic lover's spat. Who knows why it's called a spat, since spitting is the one thing you should never do—but here are some perfectly acceptable weapons:

The dis and disavow: "You suck. I wish I never met you."
The rip down memory lane: When you rip up all the photos of you together in front of her eyes.
The size revise: When she delivers the ultimate below-the-belt blow by telling you you don't exactly put the "long" in "schlong."
The flirt alert: When she tries to get you jealous by letting you know she's been flirting with someone.
Shelf destruction: Getting so pissed off that you start randomly taking things off the shelf and smashing them.

Hamper tantrum: When she throws all of your dirty clothes at you and tells you to get out.

The hell-off: "Go to hell!"

The pissper: When you whisper in a pissed-off manner because you don't want the neighbors or someone in the next room to hear.

The W bomb: Saying "whatever" to wipe out the entire conversation.

The badbye: Saying goodbye in a not-so-good way, for instance:

- **Peace-ive aggression**—Peacing her off by saying the word "peace" and leaving.
- **The sudden departyture**—Slamming the door and going out to drink with your bros.

ringlish – The language of marriage.

Even if your first language is English, you're going to have to learn a totally new one when you're putting the ring on her. Expressions like "yes, honey" and "I'm sorry, that was very insensitive of me" are going to have to become part of your vocabulary. In fact, every time you feel like saying the words *"hell* no" or "I'm not your water boy, bitch!" you may find your mouth shackled like Hannibal Lecter's. At first you'll have more trouble saying "love" than a Japanese exchange student speaking Engrish, but unless your wedding ring is a **shamrock**—a diamond that you put on her finger knowing that the marriage is a sham—you better learn fast. After all, marriage is forever, something that tends to summon up the terrifying image of those two sisters from *The Shining* saying, "Come and play with us . . . forever and ever . . . and ever . . ." Then again if you were marrying twins, you'd probably be *okay* with marriage being forever.

tittiosyncrasies – Tit-related idiosyncrasies.

If you were to open a book titled *Our Boobies, Ourselves*, you'd see many different titty types:

scareolas – Areolas that are so big it's scary.

saggie baggies – Small boobs that nevertheless sag.

flipples – Nipples that instantly "turn a girl on" when you touch them.

eraserheads – Breasts that have nipples the size of pencil erasers.

stress breasts – Tits loaded with so much silicone that they're like stress balls.

marionette set – When stretch marks cause boobs to look like they're hanging by string.

gripples – Nipples so long that you could practically grip them in a fist.

gAy-cups – A cup–sized breasts that are no bigger than man cans, making you feel gay when you play with them.

haireolas – Areolas that have boob pubes growing out of them. Women grow attached to these and even name them things like Curly Sue. Since asking her to trim is not an option, simply proceed to foreplay and while you're nibbling on her nips, discretely clip the rogue pube by securing it between your teeth and grinding down. During the afterglow, confess that you did it while you were lost in the heat of passion.

Tittiosyncracies (and of course, their nether-region equivalent, **clitiosyncracies**) are what keep us in a state of constant curiosity about women—if all breasts looked the same, they wouldn't titillate us quite so much, would they? That's why men always remain **cleavigilant**—ever on the lookout for cleavage. A "pair stare" is the only way to breastimate the size, or the **breasurements**, of the woman you're talking to. When the bra falls off, are you going to experience "knock shock" because what you thought were itty bitty titties are actually gargantuan gazoongas, or will her seemingly taught tits sag when they flop out of their boulder holders, proving to be a **floptical illusion**. There is almost nothing so depressing as seeing an unhooked bra cause sudden **cleavaporation**, but if you want to save yourself a lot of grief you'll learn not to be a **perkfectionist**.

vagibberish – Words only someone with a vagina would listen to or care about.

Just like *Peanuts* characters hear nothing but "wha wham wham whamp" when adults talk, sometimes you tune out your girlfriend when she launches into a **yawnversation** about, oh, say, the cute thing her cat did the other day. (*Jesus, she talks about that cat more than you talk about pussy!*) It's hard not to fall asleep on this kind of **snoratory**, but when your girl is delivering a **chickspearean holiloquy**, you should at least feign interest in her boring **clit chat**. Make like the NSA and tune in when there's mention of certain things, like a family member, a date such as a birthday or anniversary, or a health problem—especially if it's one you're responsible for. Be careful, though, to actually listen—don't tell her "Don't worry honey, you're not getting fat" just because you heard the word "fat." Maybe she was saying that she wants to get dinner at the Fat Cat. Next thing you know she's screeching, "So you're saying I'm too fat to eat a nice dinner?"

You should also make sure you can tell when she's two sentences away from asking a question—to do this you'll have to rely on the skills you developed in middle school: Remember how you always sensed when you were about to be called on despite the fact that you were ignoring the teacher and drawing cocks on your desk?

And of course, have stock responses ready for when you *are* called upon.

VAGIBBERISH	AUTO-RESPONSE
"blah blah blah blah. So do you think I should buy it?"	"Whatever makes you happy! You only live once!"
"blah blah blah blah. Can you believe she had the nerve to say that?"	"Incredible. So what did you say?"
"blah blah blah blah. So what would *you* do in that situation?"	"Probably exactly what you did!"

Vilentine's Day – A vile holiday in which your girl expects to be shot in the heart with an arrow and you want to be shot in the head with a bullet.

V-day is the one day of the year when a girl is sure to PMS on you no matter what time of the month it is—all you can do is throw bon bons into the lion's den in an attempt to normalize her serotonin levels. During Valentine's, a girl expects you to pull out all the stops—and that *doesn't* include the "stop nagging me about whether I'll be free that night—it's *two months from now*" or the "let's stop seeing each other." The "stops" include a prime reservation at an impresstaurant, a shower of flowers, and maybe a gift certificate to a spa so she can work off the stress brought on by endlessly harassing and haranguing you about this accursed holiday.

To cover yourself, send at least five-hundred roses to her office to insure that her vase is ten times bigger than the ones on her coworkers' desks. If you haven't turned her cubicle into a botanical garden that tells the entire office "Somebody loves me!" your two-hundred dollars in roses is just the cost of failure. Don't worry about being considered a **flowerpuss** (a pussy for getting a girl flowers), this is the one day when dudes get a pass, because it really is a matter of life and death. Many a man has suffered a St. Valentine's Massacre for failing to deliver the goods. To get through this day, just think of it as Valloween—just like Halloween except instead of dressing up as a Dick in a Box, you're playing the scary role of a romantic suitor. And the more "treats" you give her, the more likely she'll turn a trick for you at the end of the night.

Of course there's also the option of being "Valentine's gay"— when your girl's psycho behavior around the time of Valentine's drives you to swear off the opposite sex and spend the evening in the company of your best bro. Just know that "gay or stay" rules are doubly in effect for this particular night.

GUYKU #9
Valentine's Day soon.
To top last year I must find
Applebee's coupons.
—STIRLING SNOW

Wegmanesque – Just as fat chicks are said to be Rubenesque, this word refers to chicks who, like the subjects of William Wegman's photos, are total dogs.

6

CHILLOQUIALISMS

(n.) Colloquialisms specific to the art of chilling

There are times, every now and then, when bros hang out without partying down—for instance, when they're totally wiped from a night of partying down. This is called chilling like a villain—most likely a reference to Caligula, a vicious chiller who slept with his sisters and other dudes' wives before he was assassinated by some hater. Either way, whether you're chilling like Caligula or chilling with a chili dog or chilling at Chili's or chilling in Chile or chilling like you're making a killing, or even chilling on the ceiling like that chilling dead-baby scene in *Trainspotting*, you're going to need words to describe your tendency to chill for the thrill. After all, you're a Natural Born Chiller, outchilling people by a chillionfold. If you were an animal you'd be a chiller whale, or maybe Punxsutawney Chill, since you're too busy chilling to come out and see your chillhouette. You're like a chilling machine—everything you do is so chillfully executed that you're bound to become governor of Chillinois and pass a Chill Bill that gives everyone a day off just to chill. You're like Richard Chillhous Nixon, breaking up civil wars by telling people to just chill already. Is it really chilly in here? Yes indeed it is *silly* chilly because you are chilling like you're grilling a chiliburger. You are chill to the gills, popping chill pills like you have unlimited refills. You're like a chillosopher who advocates man's chill power—a regular Arthur Schopenchiller. You're the chilligitimate child of Chillary Swank and Benicio Chill Toro. You measure your energy output in chillowatt hours, and if you keep chilling then God willing, you're going to become a chillebrity who regularly appears on the cover of *Sports Chillustrated*. If you were to write your life story you'd do it on a chilluminated manuscript—you'd probably write it under the pseudonym Chillary Chillton and the title would be *It Takes Some Chillage*. Or maybe you'd fictionalize it and write a chilldungsroman rife with chilloqualisms. After all, you're a serial chiller who is dressed to chill in a chill-fitting Tommy Chillfiger suit. You're a member of the Chilluminati, and if anyone has a problem with any of this they better chill the fuck out.

Now that that's been established, let's review some methods of chilling, shall we?

carbecue – 1. "Baking" a car by lighting up a joint. 2. Trashing your old car—or someone else's—by dousing it in gasoline and setting it on fire.

chillettante – One who is a total dilettante when it comes to chilling.

chilliards – Billiards, when played for the purposes of chilling with your bros.

chill-tempered – Naturally inclined to chilling. Sometimes you're so chill-natured that you become **chillustrious**, i.e. renowned for chilling like the Dude in *The Big Lebowski*.

chip trip – 1. A trip to the convenience store to pick up chips for the game. 2. A trip to the nearest town with a casino, for the purposes of poker or other forms of gambling: "Oh you're going to Vegas—is it a chip trip or a splaycation?"

cigarsenal – Your arsenal of cigars: "I always keep a Cuban in my cigarsenal." Note that this can also include anything you keep in a cigar box, including weed, etc.

clinch mob – A drunken mob that takes to the streets after a team has clinched the pennant or a championship.

Say the Cubbies break the curse of the billy goat—you and your fellow bleacher creatures are bound to erupt into total **fandemonium**. First, you decend onto the turf and turn it into a "field of screams." Eventually cops move you into the streets where you procede to **wincinerate** everything in your path by heaving **wincendiary devices**. It's a total **winferno**! All of a sudden you find victory very uplifting—and you also find yourself uplifting a brand new Mercedes without a care in the world, despite the news cameras studiously trained on you. When you're shielded by the **fanonymity** of fifty complete strangers wearing the exact same jersey as you, why *not* go car tipping?

It's not hard to join a clinch mob. The second your team wins, leave your home and listen for the mating call of your fellow fans. You'll hear them rooting and hollering from miles away, and with the help of your **bronar** (your sonar-like ability to locate your bros) you'll have no problem joining in the post-game fellabration. Suddenly, certain previously untoward things become totally acceptable—for instance yelling in the faces of random pedestrians, **guy-fiving** everyone who walks by, and dumping Gatorade buckets on blind people. Drunk chicks will want to join in the madness and you should totally use this as an opportunity to hoist up the ones in skirts so all of your bros can catch an eyeful.

Looting is generally pointless (you just bought a $70,000 home theater system to watch the game, so you don't really need another one) but don't hesitate to participate in **de-fan-estration**—defenestrating a rival fan by throwing him through a display window.

cock shock – When you go to a party expecting a "breast fest" but walk into a meat hang: "Dude, it was a total sausage fest. I went into cock shock."

couch ouch – The pain you feel when your couch dance is over and you have to surrender your money.

crackcident – 1. A crack-related accident (see **Tampaxccident**). 2. A car or bike crash that occurs while you're staring at a girl's butt crack, sometimes called a "rearender."

Accidents happen. Sometimes because you're driving your blottomobile with a cargarita or a cartini in hand—other times because you're driving down Route 69 and you become entranced by a jogger's gluteus maximus. The next thing you know your decapitated head is lying in some bush and you have mere moments to say "Damn, that girl was *hot*" before the synapses stop firing and you're climbing the stairway to heaven. (Note: no matter how hard you ask, God will not let you sit under said stairway and look up girls' skirts).

When you see a jogger from your car, peep at her posterior but avoid being hypnotized by her curves—there might be an actual curve up ahead. Likewise, if you see a jogger coming toward you, bazongas bouncing, you might get caught in a rackcident. Even when you make it past a jiggling jogger unscathed, there's still the temptation to grab your clutch. Careful or you'll get caught in a jackcident. Sure, you'll get to ask for the chick's number—she'll have to be a witness in your manslaughter trial—but it's not worth it. Even greater are the chances of getting into a **blowlision**. When getting highway head, don't be Dill Earnhardt Jr. Maintain a manageable speed and stay straight as an arrow. Avoid hard turns. "Steady as she blows."

douchetination – A location where "the douche is loose."

Why were raver pants invented? Because some places get flooded in douche water. To avoid these spots, you must first identify them. Look for the following:

1. **A douche kebab** – A line of chickless chodes at the door.
2. **Sandwich boards** – Guys who display team logos on both a T-shirt and a backwards baseball cap. Wearing anything backwards should have ended with Kris Kross, but some think baseball hats are an exception to the rule. Maybe they need to have clear sightlines for when they inevitably get bitchslapped.
3. **Douchshades** such as Oakley sunglasses. Unless you've just

smoked some **carijuana** and are hiding your dilated pupils from the po-po, don't wear your sunglasses at night.

4. **Doucheshirts** offering "Free Mustache Rides" or identifying someone as a "Certified Sex Instructor."

5. **Shotzis** who are almost Nazi-like in their insistence that you do a Jäger bomb or a Date Rape on Campus.
6. **A "barf room" attendant** – Especially one that stocks Axe Body Spray.
7. **Bannedthems** – Anthems that even the worst wedding DJ would know not to play, such as any post-*Bad* Michael Jackson, Chaka Khan's "I'm Every Woman" (aka the Oprah theme song), Alanis Morrisette's "You Oughtta Know," or Kelly Clarkson's "Since You've Been Gone."

What are the top douchetinations in the nation? Safe to say, if the travel guide lists the Rape Crisis Center or the local abortion clinic under "Helpful Numbers," it's a douchetination. Go to places like Las Vegas or Daytona Beach on a **splaycation** and you'll end up drowning in douche water (when it rains, it pours). If you want to see boobs without being surrounded by rubes, go to the annual Sturgis rally. Bikers are kind of douchey in their own way (bandanas aren't much better than backwards baseball hats) but you'll be too much of a pussy to have that thought.

ESPNvy – A chick's jealousy over your love of ESPN.

Certain **ESPNemies** seek to **ESPNcroach** on your viewing of the Entertainment Sports Network channel, whether it's your "pigskin ignorant" best bud who wants to hit the clubs or your chick who wants you to celebrate her birthday even though you're **ESPNgrossed** in a no-hitter. Those who haven't been **ESPNlightened** have notoriously low **ESPNdurance** levels. Don't expect them to have the same amount of **ESPNergy** as you do, and be careful how you exercise your sense of **ESPNtitlement**, or your girl may put your softball bat through the television. Also, beware of **ESPNcephalitis**, a disease whereby you waste away because all you ever do is watch *SportsCenter*.

fanbulance – An ambulance that carts away an injured fan.

Even die-hards suffer the occasional "cheering impairment"— whether it's because they get hit in the face by a fly ball, or they catch the fly ball only to get hit in the face by someone who wants it. Or maybe a **fantagonist** shoves you off of the upper deck and the only thing breaking your fall is a twelve-year-old kid and his mini-helmet sundae. Maybe some **NBA-hole** you're taunting "breaks the fourth wall" by going into the crowd and then breaks your nose with his fist. Or maybe a running back gets slammed into the sidelines and the next thing you know your legs get snapped like a football after "hike."

After years of ardent cheering, your vital senses might even end up going. First you lose your vision from constantly straining to catch a glimpse of cheerleader panty. Then your hearing goes after one too many air horn blasts. Then it's sayonara to your sense of touch after you get frostbite from clutching an ice-cold Bud in football weather. Unfortunately it's very hard to lose your senses of taste and smell, meaning you're going to have to continue to put up with nasty stadium food and restrooms that are so flooded in piss that you're wondering why the president hasn't brought in FEMA.

fandiloquence – The grandiloquence of a sports fan who, though he normally has the cognitive and conversational skills of a shaved ape, suddenly becomes an eloquent statesman when **fanalyzing** his team, rattling off stats, trivia, and complicated theories like he's a member of Mensa. Football fans often show off their **NFLoquence** when engaging in **NFLocution**, and fans of every sport are apt to launch into **manageremiads**— jeremiads about how the manager needs to be fired.

fanimal – A fan who's so hardcore that he's on the verge of becoming a wild animal—as if he has taken **fanabolic steroids**. He often becomes **fanimated** to the point of fantagonizing the opposition and breeding rampant **fanimosity**.

fan tan – Literally, the tan you aquire after a day at the stadium, when you drink so much that you forget to get out of the sun—or figuratively, the pasty white skin you acquire from guybernating and watching college football all day.

fanthem – 1. A team song or **wincantation**, such as the Bears' "Super Bowl Shuffle" or the Braves' tomahawk-chop chant. 2. The song that plays for a player as he runs out to greet the fans during pre-game or steps up to the plate. 3. Melodramatic NFL Films music.

freegurgitate – To house food that's on the house, usually bar grub that's been sitting around for several days or pizza that's about to be thrown out five minutes before the slice joint closes.

fun-up – To one-up someone by bringing way more fun to the table: "I thought I was a rock star for bringing a Twister mat and some Crisco but Chuck fun-upped me by bringing a Moon Bounce and some twin sisters."

gay or stay – An expression used when deciding whether it's safe to dine or drink with your bro in a certain bar or restaurant: "I don't know man—I hear the rib eye is good here but I see a lot of candles. Gay or stay?"

Unless you're taparators (guys who operate on girls at tapas bars), you and your bro are going to want to steer clear of places with a "bag check," meaning that you give up your ballsack upon entry. Before the hostess asks how many you are, determine how *manly* you are in relation to the restaurant. When manalyzing, turn and burn if you see any of the following:

1. **Candles and dimmers.** On a first date, it's good to **dimbibe**. Flattering lighting plus booze can turn a girl who looks like Marilyn Manson into Marilyn Monroe, and it's often the only thing that keeps a "blind date" from being an "I wish I was blind date." But when you're drinking with your bro, you want the place to be even brighter than that time your mom flicked on the lights while you were yanking it.

2. **Moroccan lamps and throw pillows.** If you're at a restaurant with a fruity Moroccan theme, don't think you can save your dignity by inviting girls to toke off of your hookah—at the end of the day you're sucking on a pipe that has furry balls on it.

3. **No music or low music.** A restaurant should be loud enough that you can raise your voice a few notches and say things like "Dude, she totally wants us" without being heard by the boyfriend of the chick in question.

4. **White tablecloths.** A classic no-no. If tables *are* covered, make

sure it's by paper that you can draw gigantic cocks and balls on. Oh, and leave your digits on it for the waitress, of course.

5. **A sommelier.** Why would a restaurant hire a "wine director" when they could hire a shot girl instead? Avoid establishments with champagne buckets unless they're for Rolling Rock nips.

6. **Adjectives like this on the menu:** braised, baby (carrots, etc.), organic, all-natural, multi-grain, vine-ripened, sautéed, stir-fried, herbed, sun-dried, sun-kissed, macrobiotic, steamed, marinated, soy, heirloom, Greenmarket, and of course cruelty-free. Look out for the **shamburger**, a veggie burger that can also be called a **ma'amburger** because chicks are the only ones who'd order such a thing.

On the other hand, stay if you see:

1. **Dude lighting** – Mood lighting created by flat-screen TVs and neon Miller Lite signs.

2. **'Bate-resses** – Waitresses hot enough to fill your spank bank, obviously preferable to **overweightresses**.

3. **A "manu" featuring adjectives like:** hand-pulled, slow-roasted, triple smoked, rubbed, brined, creamed, stacked, stuffed, smothered, country-fried, chicken-fried, competition-style, beer (or bourbon) battered or braised, burnt, charred, on-the-bone, bone-in, off the slab, house cured, pickled, head-on, deep-fried, fire-kissed, bacon-wrapped, BBQ, etc. In fact words like blackened, pounded, and battered should make the menu read sort of like a domestic violence report. Always order the **glamburger**—the wildly overpriced hamburger made from a 50/25/25 mix of pork belly, Kobe beef, and bull's penis.

4. **Walls decorated by explorer maps or black and white photos of bridges, tunnels, dams, or skyscrapers being built.** A reminder that that burger didn't just magically appear in your hands—it had to be trucked in over a bridge

that was built by men who slaved away on it twelve hours a day and were probably damn hungry by quittin' time. So make yours deluxe, dammit!

5. **Mandeliers** – Chandeliers made from antlers.

6. **Animal heads and horns.** Especially ones with bras, Ray-Bans, ironic trucker caps, or beer-funnel hats on them. Bonus points for made-up animals such as the rump ape or entire stuffed animals such as a mountain lion humping a bear. Even better if you can ride the stuffed animals while they buck, and best of all if the entire restaurant is cleverly situated inside of a whale corpse.

gentertainment – Any form of entertainment that's intended for gentlemen, whether it's an ice hockey game or the "Cans Film Festival" your bro is throwing.

GUYKU #10
Not impossible
Watching Steven Seagal movie
Six times in a row
—PABLO MAURER

guybernation – Indulging in some "he time," usually to avoid the girlfriend or the bros.

There comes a time when even the most social of fellows must retreat like Superman going to the Fortress of Solitude, whether because he has a cold sore or because he gave himself an embarassing "stache gash" with his razor, or because he's checking into the Morrison Hotel (where the Lizard King let himself go) and drinking whiskey until his gut explodes. Someone who's participating in "coop therapy" will *maybe* leave the house if he sees an ad for Burger King's new breakfast sandwich, but that's about it.

If you're planning to pull a Henry David Thobro, fill out the following checklist of provisions before you go into your cave or you may end up descending into utter insanity and tucking your balls behind your legs in front of a mirror *Silence of the Lambs*–style.

- Toilet paper—Three rolls for wiping your butt, one roll for catching your nut.
- A copy of Proust's *Remembrance of Things Past* (in case you run out of toilet paper).
- Pornucopia—CROOSH.
- Gaming system of choice—CROOSH.
- GuyTunes—CROOSH.
- Thirty boxes of Hot Pockets and thirty bags of Combos. Maybe a White Castle Crave Case.
- Industrial trash can for discarded fast food wrappers you're too lazy to take out.
- Febreze Fabric Refresher so you can **guy-clean** your clothes.
- A piss bucket so you won't have to pause your video game.
- A bunch of poles so you can hang your dirty underwear on them like the flags at the UN.
- A parrot that can learn dirty words. If you find yourself wanting to eat it, it may be time to come out of **guysolation**.

guybrary – A library that establishes you as a man's man.

No **bangshuary** is complete without a handsome bookshelf showing off your favorite tomes of manly *mots*. Obviously the first thing to do when cultivating a guybrary is to purchase *Brocabulary*, the alpha book of the man canon. But what else to add? The problem with buying books with balls is that when your chick sees them, she might just get turned off and tell you, "I swore I'd never date a guy who reads Bret Easton Ellis" (feminists protested and boycotted *American Psycho* when it came out). That's why you should know exactly what to tell your bro and exactly what to tell your ho when they spot certain tomes in your guybrary.

American Psycho by Bret Easton Ellis
Tell your ho: "The protagonist is the quintessential symbol of fin-de-siècle *schadenfreude* run amuck."
Tell your bro: "Dude, you gotta read this part where Bateman forces this chick to eat a urinal cake!"

Bright Lights, Big City by Jay McInerney
Tell your ho: "Such a dispiriting portrayal of a young man losing his autonomy to vacuous self-indulgence."
Tell your bro: "Reading this makes me want to hoover some marching powder off a model's tits!"

Fear and Loathing in Las Vegas by Hunter S. Thompson
Tell your ho: "A damning indictment of America's unfettered consumer culture."
Tell your bro: "There's this hilarious part where they dose a 16-year-old chick with acid and practically deadhorse her!"

Any book by Charles Bukowski
Tell your ho: "To paraphrase the band Modest Mouse, Bukowski is fun to read, but who'd want to be such an asshole?"
Tell your bro: "Dude's my guydol."

The Gun: A Visual History
Tell your ho: "No single object, save perhaps the crucifix, is quite so fraught with historical and symbolic import."
Tell your bro: "Yo, check out the grenade launcher—*Fuckin' A!*"

The Game: Penetrating the Secret Society of Pickup Artists
by Neil Strauss
Tell your ho: "It's a sobering portrayal of socially alienated

individuals aspiring to establish a microcosm in which *they* are
the oppressors—it's very Fanonian that way."
Tell your bro: "Dude, have you heard about this thing called
'peacocking'? It gets you laid every time."

Mrs. Dalloway by Virginia Wolfe
Tell your ho: "Nobody penetrates the interior lives of her
characters—and at the same time has such an exacting eye for
exterior detail—like Ms. Wolfe does."
Tell your bro: "What the fuck? Some chick must've left that
here."

guygestion – The act of manly digestion.
In the *Joy Luck Club*, a bunch of chicks bonded over roasted
gingko nuts and other crappetizers. If that had been the *Boy
Luck Club*, there would've been some serious dude food on the
table. Guygestion is the art of coming up with killer flavor
combos to rival the all-time greats—sour cream and guac,
Oreos and pizza—and inventing new ways to stuff one kind of
food into another kind of food. It's all about coming up with
stuff that leaves you feeling **fatisfied**—fat and satisfied. For
instance:

Masserole – A massive, messy casserole assembled via stream of
conscious improvisation, called a **trashederole** when you assemble
it while trashed, and an **asserole** if it ends up tasting like ass.
Pourmaldehyde – Dispose of your gum (preferably Big League
Chew) by dropping it into your beer. It'll look like a pickled
brain floating in amber (hilarious for your date), and then when
you're done you'll have a beer gumball.
Hopsicles – Popsicles made from beer—100% more hops than
normal popsicles.
The chip bomb – A slice of Wonder Bread that's sprinkled with
potato chips and balled up into a perfect bolus of palate

pleasure. Try this with popcorn, peanut butter cups, Doritos, you name it, and turn the chip bomb into a lava rock by incorporating Cheez Whiz and microwaving. When chip bombs land in someone's flip cup, they must be eaten in their mushy state, and the cup chugged.

Fatdue – A more dudical version of fondue that consists of dipping balls of fried cheese into bacon grease.

Pizzaburgers – Two slices of pepperoni pizza used as burger buns.

Chili-cheese-bacon-burger-chilada-changa-wich-wrap – A chili cheese bacon burger, complete with buns, that is wrapped in a tortilla, smothered in sauce, and wrapped in another tortilla, at which point the entire concoction is deep fried, then sandwiched between two slices of bread and wrapped in another tortilla. Best served with fried ice cream.

A sub grinder hoagie hero po-boy – A deca-decker sandwich that originates at a deli that refers to foot-long sandwiches as subs. The meaty baton is then passed to a deli that refers to them as grinders, where more condiments, meats, cheeses, and bread are piled on. Then it's shipped to a deli that refers to them as hoagies, where still more fixins are added. It then goes to a deli that calls them heroes, and finally to one that calls them po-boys. The resulting sub within a grinder within a hoagie within a hero within a po-boy is held together with lawn-size American flagpoles instead of toothpicks. When you go to these places, just make sure you know whether to ask for "the works," "everything on it," or "all the way," or you may get ridiculed.

Fryders – Deep-fry a White Castle Slyder and you have a delicious, nutritious meat dumpling.

Besides punching someone out and using his glasses to start a fire so you can roast a wild boar on a spit, frying is the manliest way to prepare food, and short of cannibalism, **frygestion** is the burliest form of digestion. Some dudes have a strict **frydeology** about what they will or will not put in the pan, but any old chunk of meat can serve as an Unidentified Frying Object. True **afrycionados**—who are such authorities you might consider them **Fryatollahs**—know that *everything* tastes better when immersed in hydrogenated oils. But be careful about deep-frying while deep in your cups—sure, fryders make for yummy **smashedication**, but you might end up flame-broiling your house.

> Guyku #11
> *14 tons of ham*
> *Sits frozen alone waiting*
> *Cured smoked and unloved*
> —EC (written on the wall of Checkpoint Charlie's, New Orleans)

guyTunes – a music collection, often found on a **guyPod**, that's chock full of **manthems**.

Most men dump chunks at the sheer thought of an Ani DiFranco or a Sarah McLachlan song—unless of course they're Lilith Fairies, who pretend to like that sort of thing in order to impress chicks. On the other hand, manthems serve to remind us of our innate masculinity. Here's a list of manly qualities and the songs that celebrate them.

GENTLEMANLY SENTIMENT	GUYTUNES
We're great in bed...	"Superman" by Eminem
Which is why we get chicks to do things for us, like do the dishes or hang upside down on poles...	"Girls" by Beastie Boys, "Girls Girls Girls" by Mötley Crüe
But at the end of the day, we have little if any need for women...	"Bitches Ain't Shit" by Dr. Dre, "99 Problems" by Jay-Z

GENTLEMANLY SENTIMENT	GUYTUNES
Since they are suspicious psychos...	"Real Talk" by R. Kelly
Who give us STDs...	"Drips" by Eminem
And besides, we much prefer our freedom...	"Cowboy" by Kid Rock, "Ramblin' Man" by the Allman Brothers, "Wherever I May Roam" by Metallica, "Here I Go (Again on My Own)" by Whitesnake, "My Way" by Frank Sinatra
Our idea of which involves pounding beer and watching TV...	"Six Pack" by Black Flag, "More Beer" by Fear, "TV Party" by Black Flag, "All My Rowdy Friends Are Coming Over Tonight" and "Are You Ready for Some Football" by Hank Williams Jr.
Admiring our big balls...	"Big Balls" by AC/DC
And maybe occasionally biting into a skull.	"Skulls" by the Misfits
One last thing—we are hungry wolves who will rock you like a hurricane.	"Rock You Like a Hurricane" by the Scorpions

GUYKU #12
Riding her nobly
Gordon Lightfoot iPod track
Makes me laugh too much
—HUGH GALLAGHER

gymdigenous wildlife – Manimals that are indigenous to the gym.

When you're **gymcarcerated**, you collect a fair amount of **gymtelligence** about the people around you. You don't necessarily have to be a "pecker peeker" who "sizes up" guys in the locker room to know a thing or two about your fellow **gymdentured servants**—just look around and you'll see a number of recurring characters:

the flexpert – A self-appointed **gymstructor** who tells people that they're doing stretches wrong or misusing the **gymfrastructure**.

the pecsibitionist – Walks around with his pecs flexed, occasionally tweaking his nips to show you he's the tits.

Hans and Franz – Two musclebound dudes who are way too pumped up about spotting each other.

the ripster – A hipster who is trying to get ripped, but whose heart doesn't seem to be in it given his **workoutfit** of horn-rimmed glasses, Camper sneakers, and corduroy sweatpants.

the Stairmasturbator – Stares at chicks on the climbing machine in order to fill his spank bank. You don't want to use the shower after this guy.

the towelhead – Uses way more towels than he needs to.

the ugly red sweater– Looks like he's about to keel over because he's beet-red and pouring sweat like Ron Jeremy.

the locker gawker – Creepily looks you over while you're undressing. Even worse is the locker talker who asks stuff like, "Nice! Trim those yourself?"

the treadMILF– A chick whose hot bod you admire from behind, but when she gets off the treadmill and turns around, you see she's old enough to be someone's mother.

Shortsenegger – Wears overly revealing shorts, like Arnie circa *Pumping Iron.*

the gymposter – Shows up just to be able to tell people he goes to the gym, but doesn't do much besides sit at the juice bar hitting on the counter chick.

highorities – Your priorities for getting high: "Dude, what are our highorities here? Coke or weed? White socks or green pants? Or should we wear our white socks *with* our green pants?"

jack slacks – Pants that you wear to a strip club in order to truly milk the experience. Unless you're someone like Joey Buttafuoco, these are usually pants you'd never wear in public, such as track pants or **Cumbros** (Umbros worn for the specific purpose of coming). "Dude, you might want to change. This club is classy, they're not going to let you in wearing jack slacks."

mansportation – Transportation of a manly nature.

When you head out on the highway, do it the *guy* way. Bang a chick in your Shaguar. Show off your exquisite taste by riding a Snaab. **Nadvertise** in a Ferrari Testosterossa. Or exude hip-hop cred in an Impresscalade. You'll have no trouble landing dogs in a Land Rover—it's a regular "ho moving vehicle." But chicks are likely to avoid you if you're in a Dodge. Don't get caught in a "pride ride," a car such as a Jokeswagon that inadvertently shows off your gay pride. **Shehicles** such as Geo Jisms are strictly for the ladies. And never pick up a date in a **shoddomobile** such as a broke-down Sadillac or a barely mobile Slowyota.

The biggest no-no of all is the "wanker tanker." It's the logical outcome of Carwinism—the belief that only the fittest, most pimped-out cars survive. In 1992, Arnold Schwarzenegger bought the first civilian Hummer, and eventually super-sized it to a campaign bus called the Gropemobile. In 2005 Ashton Kutcher went truck wild by buying the first seven-ton International CXT. Then there's the most trucked-up individual: John Madden, commander of the Maddencruiser. Truck Norrises aside, the Hummer stretch limo is without a doubt today's most popular "tool bus"—the rank amateurs who tool around in it all night often hit the minibar way too hard and turn it into a "retch limo."

maximum cockupancy – When a party is full of dudes: "Bro, this party is a big box of cocks. The room is at maximum cockupancy." When this happens, immediately focus your honar so you can go from bags to bitches.

Stripley's Believe It or Not – Unusual acts and extraordinary feats occurring at a strip club; also known as stupid stripper tricks.

What's the big deal about the Indian dude with the four-foot fingernails in the *Guinness Book of World Records*? At Sweet Dreams, there's a chick named Destinee who has nails that long, *plus* she can shimmy up a ten foot pole, do a backflip that would make Shamu jealous, and hit every known pilates, yoga, ballet, karate, and Kama Sutra position on her way down, all the while vacuuming up ones, clapping her butt to Nelly, and singing, "Strip-ity-doo-da, stripity-ay!"

Starting with the midget waitress, a strip club should be a veritable three-pole circus that has you constantly wondering, "Wow! Is that real or fake!?"—and not just about the boobs. Just like your girlfriend thinks she should be able to take you to a Mark Ruffalo movie and ask you why you can't be more like him, you should be able to take her to Twisted Sisters and say, "Why can't your ass cheeks play ping pong with each other like that girl's can?"

Some other popular pole positions:

grip and strip – Taking clothes items off while on the pole. Tip: $2

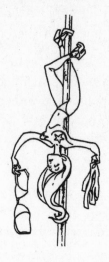

the slide and wide – Sliding down the pole while spreading 'em wide. Tip: $1

Batwoman – Hanging from the pole upside down. Tip: $2
the squirrel – Crawling down the pole headfirst. Tip: $1

the twirlie girlie – Twirling around the pole while sliding down. Tip: $1

the chunky monkey – A **Strippopotamus** who you thought was way too heavy to shimmy up a pole gets up to the rafters in five seconds flat. Tip: $3

the drop and chop (aka the guillotine) – When a woman drops directly onto the crotch of a man sitting below, threatening to snap his tool in two. Tip: Nothing if it's you, $10 if it's your friend.

the Coinstar – When you put some ones in a stipper's thong and she spits out change. Tip: "Keep the change, baby."

strippercratic oath – A stripper's obligation not to tell anyone— especially your wife—what happened in the "skeet suite."

teebauchery – Hijinks that occur on the golf links, or around a *Golden Tee* machine.

Golf has always been "a gentleman's game"—that's why when your caddie refreshes your tumbler of Everclear, you should tip him graciously, regardless of the fact that you're so wasted you could drown in a water hazard.

Guys participate in teebauchery because their golf bag, with its many compartments and its intimidating location in the garage, is often where they hide their weed stash, their porn mags, and those little airplane bottles of Johnnie Walker that get them through their morning commute. When all of these things end up on the golf course, with nary a nagging girlfriend or wife in sight, it's only natural to match each tee shot with a tequila shot. Soon you're taking a break from your Vardon grip to show the boys your hard-on grip. You've become a total **teetard**.

When "driving drunk," calculate your **slammedicap** (a type of handicap which puts you on equal footing with your more sober opponents) by taking your gross score and then subtracting the course rating as well as each shot of booze you had before or during the game.

Be aware that golfing while quaffing increases the likelihood of **parguments**—heated exchanges about whether your bro is keeping score accurately. A game of golf is like a handy in that every stroke counts, and when your bro starts fudging numbers and going back on bets, you'll have no choice but to pull a *Falling*

Down by busting out a shotgun and saying, "Now you're going to die wearing that stupid little hat."

whorescent lighting – The low, sometimes fluorescent strip club lighting that makes everything look better—except for your chronic dandruff. It also makes it hard to tell whether the girl in front of you is a man or a woman, but maybe that's for the best. When a strip club has **ultra-vile lighting** you're inevitably haunted by a panapoly of C-section scars, hail damage (also known as **'ttock pocks**), and cellublight. In fact, when the lights are up, you might experience **stripecac**—an instance of stripping that reveals a body that's outright nauseating.

wintimacy – The intimacy that is established between two total strangers when their team wins.

When someone hits a game-winning homer, you're likely to grab the nearest dude, no matter who he is, and become "homer homos," embracing in a way that is nothing short of **homer-erotic**. You **wintroduce** yourself to everyone wearing your team's jersey, buy them shots, and give them guy-fives. It's important that you don't let this dudephoria turn into outright **winsolence**, since taunting fans of the losing team might lead to a neanderbrawl, and subsequent **wincarceration**. Celebrating a grand slam is never worth a night in the slammer.

7

SPANKSPEAK

(n.) The handiest words of all

As Dr. Phil says, "You have to love yourself before someone can love you." So true, dude, so true! Good things come to those who 'bate. And yet, having sex with someone you love, as the aptly named Woody Allen put it, has long been a taboo. If you talk about jerking it, you're considered a jerk—a real wack job. Tell someone you like to beat it and they'll tell you to beat it. Over the years, bater-haters have gone to great lengths to avoid referring to **hand-to-glans combat** by name. They called it "self-pollution," "self-abuse," and "secret vice" while claiming it led to insanity—which explains why asylum inmates have to have their hands tied to their chest. Luckily things have changed since Immanuel Kant wrote that "calling such a vice by its proper name is considered a kind of immorality." These days, countless expressions pertain to choking the chicken, but pretty much all of them describe the act of pounding the flounder in simple terms. They ignore the fact that pulling the pud is something dudes do for a variety of reasons, in myriad ways, everywhere from a jack shack in Iraq (Anthony Swofford) to a porno theater near mom's house (Pee-wee Herman).

Only by coming up with a wider array of jerking jargon can we get a firm grip on this sticky subject.

dicksturbing – Describing the state of surprise that occurs when you unexpectedly see another man's member, especially when it's larger or smaller than you previously considered possible.

doppelwanger – A porn star who has a wang that looks exactly like yours, making it easy to consider him your doppelbanger and live **vagicariously** through him.

EMS (Emergency Manual Stimulation) – A hand job or auto-erotic sesh that occurs for the purposes of revival. "Oh man, I have the worst hangover. I think I need some EMS."

fasturbation – Having to masturbate at an accelerated rate, either because your girl is about to get out of the shower or because you have to leave for work in five minutes or the airplane you're on is going down. Usually comes in the form of **half-masturbation**, when your pants are at half-mast (halfway down your legs) so you can pull them up easily if necessary.

frusterbation – Masturbating because you've been blue-balled or sexually frustrated: "The date was a complete **jizaster**—I ended up going home and frusterbating until my schlong was rawer than Eddie Murphy."

jerkumstantial evidence – Evidence that you've jerked it, such as wadded tissues or BeautiesWithBooties.com left up on your skinternet browser. If a girl asks you to explain jerkumstantial evidence such as some Charmin that you've been harmin', just say, "I had the stiffles, er, sniffles."

masturdate – An auto-erotic session that has been planned in advance, like a date.

Masturdates are much like real dates, except that in this case you're taking *yourself* out, and dinner and a movie means a bag of Cheez Puffs and *The Nuttin' Professor* on DVD.

These romantic rendez-yous usually revolve around a specific occasion: Say, the GF has planned a girls' night out for the end of the week, finally leaving you with the two hours it takes to inflate, boff, and deflate that Stacy Layne doll.

menstrubating – Masturbating because your menstruating girl-friend doesn't want to have sex, or you don't want to "go with the flow." Known as a **rag jag** if she jags you off while she's on the rag.

phallywacker – One who wacks his tallywacker.

phonanism – Engaging in onanism while on the phone.

While this can refer to phone sex, it also applies to the act of stroking yourself anytime you're "on the horn," even if it's just with the chick who called to ask you why you're having trouble making the minimum payment. She runs down a list of options and by the time she reaches unsecured consolidation loan, you've made a large deposit into some Kleenex. If a cold caller gets you hot, it's very rare that you'll have enough time with her to do the deed, even if you're **fasturbating**. Try pretending English is your second language and ask her to speak slowly and repeat herself a lot.

porn-on date – The "born-on date" of a porno: "Dude, look at that guy's mullet—what the hell is this thing's porn-on date!" "I'm thinking late 70s?" "Dude, this is *before-I-was-bornography*!"

procrasturbation – Masturbation that occurs for purposes of procrastination.

Set up a home office and you'll inevitably end up using your work station as a jerk station. Why do you think your boss won't let you work from home? He knows you're more likely to fill up TP than fill in TPS reports.

When getting work done is like pulling teeth, *don't* resort to pulling skin. "Nut breaks" are *not* the solution. Instead hold out, get the job done, and *reward* yourself with some **congratubation**. Write that fifty-page prospectus and then sit back and say, "I really gotta hand it to myself."

the porning after – Waking up, turning on your computer, and being ashamed to see what you were pounding it to the night before.

pornocopia – A cornucopia (or "*horn*-o-plenty") of pornography, known as a **jack stack** if it's a stack of **jagazines**; a **jack crack** if it's a crack between mattresses where you stash your porn; and a **slapper keeper** if for some reason you keep your porn in a three-ring binder. The age-old term for a desktop computer that stores such material and the "work station" around it is, of course, a **jerk station**—it's where you work your fingers to the bone.

reality jack – A reality check that occurs via jacking off.

Does making a move on your best bro's girl seem like a good idea? Thinking about booty-calling your psycho-clingy ex-girlfriend? Before you do anyone drastic, remember that at times excess semen floods our brains, causing synapses to misfire and making us mistake bad ideas for good ones. That's when it's time to **elimibate** those bad impulses. Once you've beaten those excess fluids back, you'll realize you were seeing the world through **aroused-colored glasses**, and you'll thank yourself for keeping a "level head."

Reality jacks aren't just something you give to yourself in order to avoid doing your dog in a desperate moment. Let's say you're making love to the old lady: Screwrette's kicks in and you feel inexplicably compelled to scream out "Want! To! Marry! You! Let's! Start! Family!" Before you say anything **ricockulous**, wait for her to finish you off—chances are, when she's done going down on you, you won't be thinking about going down the aisle with her.

scornography – Porn that you scorn in public but watch in private. Sometimes called **tornography** because although you feel morally torn, you can't tear yourself away from it.

smashedurbation – Masturbation while you're smashed (alternately— **obliderbation**, masturbating while you're obliterated; or **plaster-bation**, masturbating while you're plastered). Smashedurbation can sometimes lead to a jackout, i.e. blacking out while you're jacking off. If you're far gone with a hard-on, make sure to do the deed in a locked room that can't be accessed by your frat brothers, or pictures of you passed out with your ass out may end up all over the net. Also, heed the Spermin' General's Warning: Passing out on your arm can be deadly. Break it and your only onanistic option will be **plaster-casturbation**.

spankrupt – Unable to spank it anymore due to the fact that you've polished your knob like O. J. Simpson sitting around polishing his Heisman; a sign that you just might be a **jerkaholic**.

tear jerking – Jerking it while crying. Usually occurs while you're watching **mournography**—amateur porn you filmed of an ex-girlfriend whose loss you're still mourning.

tittieotape – A videotape containing titties—often a homemade sex tape, also known as a **cockumentary**.

tug of war – When you tug on your "hardly-on" as if you're at war with it. Usually involves a lot of **tug talk** such as, "Come on, buddy . . . time to get nutty . . ."

8

SHITTER CHATTER

(n.) Shit talk

E ver since the first caveman saw a fossilized dinosaur dropping and said, "What is this shit?" turd words have been ubiquitous, and it's no mystery why. As men, we're taught to be proud of our accomplishments, and long before we make our first million on the stock market, we make our first doodoo in our diapers. That's why when you say something is awesome, you say it's *"the shit."*

And yet neither your boss nor your girlfriend are impressed when you cock-a-doodle-doo about caca and doo-doo. Girls just don't take the same delight in talking about shite. It might be because they drop **hamsturds**—turds that are so small and bolus-like that it looks like a hamster squeezed them out. They'd rather sweep the whole subject under the rug. Between your girl turning up her nose and your colleagues acting like their stuff don't stink, you might start feeling that in life, nobody likes a shitter.

So who shares your philosophy of "carpe BM"? Well your bros, of course—they understand that a doodie is a thing of beauty. When you tell them to come admire a deposit you just made in the tank, they're always willing to be "bowled over." In a perfect world, we'd all have motorized port-a-potties of the sort used in an outhouse derby, in which we could tool around and show our stool around. However as things now stand, the only way we can share our shits is by using **poo-phemisms**. There are thousands of these expressions—everything from the old-as-shit "track marks" to the more recent "Cleveland Steamer"—and new ones plop up all the time. Still, the author of this book wants to leave his mark by adding to the **turdminology**. So let's plunge right in!

deuceappear – To disappear in order to drop a deuce; split and shit.

During certain situations where your presence is of the utmost importance (say, during a first date), you retire to the restroom to squeeze out what at first you think will be a simple "fresh-start fart," but before you know it you're committing **involuntary canslaughter**. The second you start turning the bowl into a World War II atoll, you realize you better get your boxing gloves on because you're about to "dook it out." While you succumb to **cryarreah** (a dump that's so trying it causes you to break down weeping), your date is fiddling with her wineglass wondering where the hell you are. "What is this shit?" she's thinking, "Something smells funny here." Soon she decides she's had enough of this crap—she tells herself you're an asshole that doesn't give two shits about her, and a sense of relief washes over her as she plops her credit card down. Meanwhile you're laying brownstones with the fervor of a late nineteenth-century row-house builder. You look in the bowl and it's a veritable confederacy of deuces. You tell your bunghole, "You're doing a heck of a job, Brownie." But by the time you return to the dining room your date is gone and you've suffered the most humiliating of all fates—you've been dumped while taking a dump.

It's one thing to hit the shitter to relieve first-date jitters, but quite another to put your job at risk by spending Willy Wonka–like time in the chocolate factory. You'll never get ahead spending so much time on the head, and sudden deuceappearances can put a serious black mark on your professional record. Make too many direct deposits in the company restroom and you can easily go from being "the shit" to being in deep shit—next thing you know your career is in the tank. It's as easy as missing a single conference call because you were in the stall. Sure, you can try to stall for time, flush-faced, when your boss asks you where you were, but when all is spread and done, you won't be sitting pretty. Your boss will continue unloading on you, threatening to take you to the cleaners if you keep staining the company's reputation.

And then the fateful day will come when your pants fall and the axe falls. Getting canned on the can is everyone's worst shitemare. No sooner have you found an empty stall and said, "Stallelujah!" than your boss comes into the restroom and says, "Clean out your bowels and then clean out your desk. Clean off the brown and take the next bus out of town. That's right—wipe up and ship out!" You'll try to make him see reason while you keep on squeezin', but even before you've finished the roll, he'll say, "You're head's going to roll. Wipe your crack—you've just been sacked. I gave you a shot, but you spent too much time on the pot." And you'll be shit out of luck. To make sure things don't go down like this, wait till you have a good **plopportunity**—i.e. your boss is gone for lunch and you can relieve yourself without him getting wind of it.

Another shitty thing to do is to deuceappear during a **broccasion**. Don't binge on **bromestibles** such as Frito-Lay pies while you're watching the game at your bro's pad or you may end up turning his **pied-a-terre** into a **pied-a-merde**—meaning, you may turn his starter studio into a farter studio. It stinks, but once an apartment has become an **afartment**, there's squat-all you can do about it except issue an earnest **crapology**.

Abandoning the Super Bowl so you can use the pooper bowl is a shitty thing to do—especially if you're the only other person watching it with your bro. If a linebacker falls out of bounds and only one man is there to see it, did the linebacker really fall out of bounds? Sure, you can always run into the living room for the instant replay, but do you really want to do the Super Bowl

Shuffle with your pants around your ankles? Is catching that end-zone sack really worth showing off your sack?

Of course, sometimes you just have to tell your bro, "Tough shit, I'm taking a dump." That's fine, but at least have the courtesy to wear a **stall shawl**—take your shirt off and wrap it around your shoulders to keep it from absorbing the stink. After a bowel movement at the movies, always take a walk to clear your hind. Same if you're on a date—telling her you were on the phone shooting the shit with a client isn't going to fly if you return to the table emitting gag-inducing "tail fumes." Clear the air down there or she may never talk to you again.

People will also deuceappear to make a "stall call." Look, it's no biggie to engage in polite "shitter chatter" with your fellow restroom users but have you ever walked in to hear some anonymous chotch loudly using his phone on the throne? Don't hesitate to flush these PDA-holes out of the next stall, loudly apologizing after each courtesy flush—"Sorry about the tank stank, buddy!" Or initiate a "cough-off"—when two dudes in a restroom trade coughs, snorts, loogie hocks, and other expectorations to see who's the Archduke of Dooks. Hopefully you'll disrupt his conversation to such a degree that he'll run away with his pants around his ankles.

As you know, when someone is in your **immediate pissinity**— i.e. standing at the urinal next to yours—you have a choice between the **thousand-tile stare** (staring straight ahead at the wall tiles in a zen-like trance) or the **pants-down glance down** (fixing your gaze on your own member). When the urinals have no privacy barrier, you're obliged to employ the thousand-tile stare, lest your neighbor think you're giving him a "glans glance." When there *is* a privacy barrier, it's a matter of personal preference.

Don't underestimate the importance of these rules. Having bad headiquette can cost you your job, or at the very least your dignity. If you become "gun shy" and dry up every time the boss is in your immediate **pissinity**, carry a squirt bottle of lemon juice every time you head to the head, so you can at least simulate a power pee. Your boss might wonder why your whiz smells like lemonade, but at least he'll respect you as a man.

Some dudes are **crapprehensive** about every tiny thing that happens in the restroom. Like sensitive plants, they can only crap under the proper conditions. They'll "stall for time" until the other person leaves the restroom, just to avoid being caught with their pants down. It's animal nature to establish one's dominance in these situations, so hit the head with your head held high. Don't be a **stallflower**—the guy who uses the stall instead of the urinal to take a piss. Employ a power stance not only at the urinal, but also on the john. The guy in the next stall should be able to see his reflection in your wingtips.

Then there's the matter of shitterature—toilet reading you carry into the stall. It's natural to want to get the poop while taking a poop, and to that end you'll often find yourself reading the *Stall Street Journal*—a respected publication that has repeatedly won the Stoolitzer Prize for offering breaking news to people who are breaking wind. It's also common to take a rolled-up magazine, or a **bowl scroll**, into the crapper at work—just know that it's your doody duty to pass the baton to the next person who uses the toilet.

Follow these rules and you'll be shitting pretty. And remember, at the end of the day the most important thing is that you leave the toilet with a sense of **shatisfaction**.

fartisan – One who takes pride in the art of the fart; a real "stall star."

fart-to-fart – A **fartwarming** experience in which two dudes trade farts.

flyarrhea – A case of diarrhea so bad that it causes you to jet, also known as **seeyarrhea** or **goner-rrhea**. ("Dude, what happened to you the other night? You disabeered from the bar." "Oh man, those nachos gave me a bad case of flyarrhea. I had to get home fast—it was a real **brownpour**.")

group farticipation – When an entire group participates in a veritable fart orgy.

Not every night with your bros can involve passing a girl around—sometimes you just sit around passing gas. You're watching the game when someone issues a "fart of war"—a gastardly "fart attack" that triggers **guyological warfare**. Next thing you know, another dude has a "momentary lapse of squeezin'." The room becomes polluted with "air farticles"—it's a virtual gas chamber. The only way to get a leg up on the enemy is to commit "flatulatory rape." Pummel him with stink bombs until your own reek prevails. Now you're cooking with gas! And don't hesitate to fight dirty—just make sure you don't suffer "fart failure" by sharting yourself.

on the pot on the dot – An expression that indicates that you made it to the toilet just in time to avoid sharting or puking all over yourself.

overplopulate – To overfill a toilet bowl: "Dude, do you have a plunger? I blew up the bowl with a **Stallotov cocktail** and now I'm having an overplopulation problem."

pissinfectant – Piss that's sprayed against a surface, such as in the case of a **murinal** (a mural made from urine): "Excuse me gentleman, but I need to pissinfect this wall."

pissticuffs – A fight resulting from or incorporating urine.

pisstracted – Distracted by an overwhelming need to piss.

plopperazzo – Someone who photographs freshly plopped turds with the fervor of a paparazzo photographing Madonna.

Just like a proud papa photographs his newborn baby, it's only natural for a proud plopper to snap a few of the turd stew he has just prepared while saying, "Now this is some good shit." Until recently, people who wanted to TM their BMs kept their photos in Crapper Keepers, but in this digital age they're able to instantly send **plop shots** to friends with a message that says "check this shit out." In fact technology has become so advanced that Fartin' Scorseses can even film **plopumentaries** with their phones, or they can record themselves taking the world's longest piss and send it to their bros in "streaming video."

stallternative – An alternative to the toilet stall. You usually have to find one when the only stall has been **overplopulated**: "Dude, the coal bowl is out of order, but those bushes are looking like a good stallternative."

PRAISEOLOGY

(n.) Phraseology that can be used to praise all that is good in this world

Life is full of stuff to get stoked about, which is exactly why Bill & Ted used words like excellent, most excellent, triumphant, outstanding, stellar, sterling, awesome, unprecedented, unrivaled, bodacious, and non-heinous. Of course, the tradition of praising stuff to your bro goes back farther than Bill and Ted or Wayne and Garth using "excellent," and even farther than Robin saying stuff like "Holy random-ass bullshit, Batman!" and yes even further back than the first caveman who thought to use a rock as a poker table, causing his bros to say, "Rock!" In fact it goes all the way back to the Bible, when God created man and saw that it was good.

Unforch, nothing sounds more painfully outdated than a passé item of praiseology—remember when peeps used "bad" to mean "good"? That was a pretty bad call—and not in a good way. Other words like fly, hype, dope, proper, and mad cool are also highly Q—highly questionable. "Hot" was taken out of commish by Nicole and Paris. As for "jiggy"—Diddy did it. Certain words like "sweet" are still pretty sweet; "choice" is still a good choice; and you should still have the A-bomb (awesome) in your arsenal if you're going to be considered a supershowerer of praise—but it's clear that more lauditory language is needed. So let's hotstep in that direction, shall we?

atrawesome – Atrociously awesome.

blechtacular – Spectacular in a disgusting or vomit-inducing way.

ferawesome – Ferociously awesome.

Flyatollah – The king of being fly.

guydol – A guy that you idolize, perhaps excessively.

George Costanza called it a "non-sexual crush," but having a hero doesn't make you homo. Well, unless someone like Lance Bass happens to be your hero—that's kind of gay.

Your early guydols will include He-Man, Superman, and others. By adolescence you've moved on to other men in tights—rock stars like Bret Michaels or sports stars like Joe Montana. Obviously the real men are the ones who roll into work wearing leotards and pants enhancers.

A guydol need not hold your awe over the course of a lifetime, or until he's traded to another team. It can also refer to a one-time occurrence: "Dude, you burned a bar down by setting fire to a mescal worm? You're my guydol!"

Men are usually guydolized for their machievements—i.e. macho achievements. These might include:

1. Being the first to land on a new planet—and hooking up with an alien.
2. Breaking the home run record—then hooking up with the chick who caught the ball.
3. Beating a professional female wrestler despite the fact that you don't even work out—then hooking up with her despite the fact that she's a lesbo.

Beware, though—guydolizing the wrong dude will count against you when you're being manalyzed. No one's going to buy the fact that you keep posters of David Beckham in your room just because you admire the way he "bends it." Here's a handy chart so you can see who should be your hero and who should be your zero.

ACCEPTABLE GUYDOLS	FALSE GUYDOLS
Hockey players	Ice skaters
Hard drinkers like Bukowski	Deep thinkers like Plato
Firemen (in the sense of talented relief pitchers)	Firemen (in the sense of shirtless dudes on calendars)
Veterans	Veterinarians
Willie Nelson	The guys from Nelson
Bob Dylan	Dylan from 90210
Hunter S. Thompson	The Thompson Twins
Benny Hill, womanizer	Benny Hinn, proselytizer
Stevie Ray Vaughan	Billy Ray Cyrus
Michael Jordan, he of "Hang Time"	Jordan Knight, he of "Hangin' Tough"
Elmore Leonard	Leonard Nimoy
Tony Soprano	A Tony-winning male soprano

nadmirable – Admirable because it took some serious nads: "Dude you told your boss to suck it? Nadmirable!"

nadvantageous – Something that's advantageous to your balls: "It would be nadvantageous for you to shut the fuck up."

perb, perior, preme – Expressions used to indicate that something is superb, superior, or supreme

Dudes who get tired of saying "awesome" sometimes shorten it to "awes," but there's something lame about that—it's almost as bad as dudes who say "obvi" as in "obvi I have no balls"! Try saying "perb" instead. "Perb" is a shortening of "superb" that's just a lot of fun to say: "Dude, you got laid? Perrrrb!"

After the initial joy of using "perb" wears off, you'll want to switch it up, and that's when you should take other "super" words and just use the last syllable. "Perior" refers to something that's superior, and "preme" refers to something that's supreme.

PERB	PERIOR	PREME
Eating a Philly cheesesteak.	Eating a Philly cheesesteak while getting a beej.	Getting a beej from the counter-girl in a cheesesteak restaurant, who gives you a $50 gift certificate.
Winning the lottery.	Finding out you've won the lottery while you're on a first date, and the girl gives you a congratulatory beej.	Finding out you've won the lottery while you're at a bar, and like nine girls give you congratulatory beejs throughout the course of the night, then when you go to close your tab the waitress says "It's on me." And gives you a congratulatory beej.
A random hot girl smiles at you on the street.	A random hot girl stops you on the street and asks if you want to exchange numbers.	You exchange numbers with a random hot girl on the street. When you call her, some other girl answers and says you have the wrong number, but would you like to come over anyway? Right after you're done with her, the hot girl calls and says she just realized she accidentally gave you her sister's number, and she wants you to come over. The girl you're with says, "Don't leave without this $50 gift certificate. I'm the manager of a cheesesteak restaurant."

PERB	PERIOR	PREME
Watching the game from a luxury suite.	Watching the game from a luxury seat with a hot chick by your side.	Watching the game from a luxury suite. Robert Redford peeps the hot chick you're with and offers you $1 million for a beej from her. You tell him you're not sure and he tells you he'll throw in a tray of cheesesteaks, hot off the grill.

threediculous – Three times as ridiculous as something that's ridiculous.

totally awessible – Something that's totally possible and would be totally awesome if it happened.

THE RIGHTEOUS BRO

aighteous – all right and righteous

courighteous – courageous and righteous

delighteous – delightfully righteous

dynomighteous – righteous enough to make JJ say "Dy-no-mite!"

exciteous – excitingly righteous

flighteous – fly and righteous

frighteous – frightfully righteous

mighteous – mightily righteous

outrighteous – outrageously righteous; outright righteous

outofsighteous – out of sight and righteous

quiteous – quite righteous

strighteous – strikingly righteous

tighteous – tight and righteous

uprighteous – righteous enough to make you stand up and cheer

white hot lighteous – so righteous it's like you died and went to Heaven

10

SPURNACULAR

(n.) A vernacular that can be used to spurn the dumbass mofos of the world

Without hate speech, there'd be no reason to go to a baseball game, since you'd have nothing to say to the left-fielder about his mother. Put-downs have been part of the male lexicon ever since "numbskull" was coined in the 1600s and "numbnuts" was coined sometime thereafter. Words like this are so crucial to guy talk that the word "boob," meaning an idiot, was coined way before "boob" meaning a bouncing booby.

In a certain sense, it's good to use outdated spurnacular, since insulting someone in a retarded way tells them that they're even more retarded than the retard who is calling them out. It's like the pothead calling the dickhead wack. That's why joking about a guy's mother cuts so close to the bone—obviously, the guy knows you didn't do his mom like you're claiming, but he can't stand the thought that his mother would give it up for someone as douchetacular as you.

A proper insult will cause someone to simultaneously want to punch you in the face but also realize that they'd lose face if they did so. Just think of every movie in which a dork has ever insulted a jock in front of a hot girl, causing the jock to walk away saying, "I'll get you next time . . ." That's when you've literally shut someone down, turning them into a "gimp chimp" without mental or physical capacities. Not that some people won't punch you in the face anyway!

With words like these you can voice your scorn for everything that's wrong with the world, starting with douchebags.

arrivedouchey – A variant of the Italian expression "arrivederci," used when you're peacing a douchebag.

assaulter ego – The part of you that just wants to beat the shit out of someone: "Your honor, ladies and gentleman of the jury— when this chode made a joke about my dead mother, he totally touched off my assaulter ego."

bagamuffin – A douchebag who dresses as poorly as a raga-muffin.

Not every chotch was born with a silver poon in his mouth— some are "nouveau douche." They spend most of their lives as rat-faced rejects but as soon as some hot chick throws them a bone, they get an unnatural sense of their own cock stock and buy a one-way ticket to Doucheville. Trouble is, they haven't learned the finer aspects of douchedom, like having a perfectly starched collar and a baseball cap that's twisted at just the right angle.

Bagamuffins are a prime example of **stooper scoopers.** They troll the douchewaters for what more attractive chodes have cast away, resembling catfish with their soul patches and goatees. These Steve Douchemis are usually pursued by girls tired of having their hearts popped like so many Tommy Hilfiger collars. They think a guy will be more sensitive, or easier to hold on to, because he looks like Nick Nolte's mug shot. Jump-cut to: The Douchemi handing her a McDonald's napkin and telling her to wipe the jiz off her face on her way home.

Douchemis can be recognized by the following:

1. **A skateboard.** Instead of paying for the girl's ride home he makes her hail it and latches onto the back for a free ride to the house of the next girl he's going to bang.
2. **A must-not-stache.** Not even the most thorough **grinspection** will tell you whether he's a herpitrator.
3. **Guyliner.** When did rock stars start wearing more make-up than porn stars?
4. **Limited-edition Nikes.** Just like Jimmy Choos are the most damning item of ho couture, vintage Jordans are a dead giveaway that someone is a **swoosh douche**.
5. **Affected love of rap music.** If a wanksta quotes lines like "bitches ain't shit but hos and tricks," maybe it's *not* necessarily because he has an admirable love of African-American culture or an endearing sense of irony.
6. **Wristbands.** Because he can't afford a chotch watch.
7. **Guyhilism.** He quotes Nietzsche to explain why the chick should pick up the bill or give him a beej.

bagvertise – To actively show everyone what a douchebag you are: "Dude, those frosted tips are a total bagvertisement."

beach bleach – Something that causes sand to become whiter than it already is, namely a pale-ass brofo: "Dude, how are we going to have a proper splaycation if you're bleaching the beach in that tiny **dickini**?" If you're worried that chicks are going to question your maleness because of your paleness, forget the beach and hit the slopes for a little **skibauchery**.

binge thinker – Someone who thinks about things too much: "Yes, we could get arrested and kicked out of college for stinking up the chancellor's office with this dead fetal pig, but don't sweat it. Stop binge thinking."

blowtesque – A way to describe something that hideously blows.

boregonzola – Something that's boring and cheesy: "That romantic comedy was 100%, USDA-approved boregonzola. I made it clear to her that dragging me to it meant she had a **blow jobligation**."

breathuselah – Someone who's breath smells like it hasn't been freshened since the days of Methuselah.

catheter – Someone who is worse than a pain in the ass; they're a pain in the dick.

chimplant – A brain implant that causes you to think and act like a chimp: "Dude, stop hooting and hollering over that stupid shit. It's like you got a chimplant."

choderiforous – Emitting an odor of unwashed chode. Can be used literally ("Dude, when are you going to change those pants? They're getting a little choderiforous.") or figuratively to indicate the behavior of a total chode warrior: "Whoa, after those douchéticles walked into the room it got very choderiforous in here."

doppeldouche – A douche who looks just like another douche. "Check out the dude with the tweezed eyebrows and frosted tips—he's Lance Bass's doppeldouche."

douché – Said when someone unexpectedly out-douches you by doing the douchiest thing imaginable: "I thought I was a tool for wearing a Polo shirt to this party, but you really 'took it up a chotch' by wearing one *and* popping the collar. Douché!"

douchebauchery – Debauchery as perpetuated by douches. Debauchery has been around forever—when man invented the wheel, the first thing he did was wheel in a keg and throw a three-day cave rave. Debauchery is all well and good so long as you make sure it doesn't cross the line into douchebauchery. That's when you and your bros have reached the point in the evening where you're too **broblivious** to realize that no woman—even a crack whore who notices a Benjamin dangling out of your back pocket—would go anywhere near you.

Even worse, you want to make sure you aren't participating in **dorkbauchery**, the kind of hedonism perpetrated by nerd herds. Use the chart below to determine which side of the fence you're on.

DOUCHEBAUCHERY	DORKBAUCHERY
You go to the club with your bros and fail to pick up chicks.	You go to the chess club with your bros and fail to pick up checkers.
You drink till you reach your boiling point and start shit with people.	You drink till you reach your "soiling point" and start shitting on people.
You all end up at one of the guys' apartments asking a chat-room girl to show T&A.	You all end up at one of the guys' apartments asking a chat-room guy to play D&D.
You get into a loud bargument about who's hotter, Venus or Serena.	Which is hotter, Venus or Mercury? (It's Venus, even though Mercury is closer to the sun.)

A sure sign that someone is engaging in douchebauchery is that the douchecibel levels have risen. **Douchecibels** are units of sound used to measure noise made by douchebags.

Boys like to make noise, and when you get a lot of douchebags together in one place it won't take long till the volume level goes through the roof and even God up in heaven above is saying, "Shut the fuck up—I'm trying to watch *Frasier*." But telling a bunch of drunk dudes to pipe down is a dicey proposition—you may end up getting clocked in the head (or even worse, Glocked in the head depending on who you're dealing with). That's why it's important to have an understanding of douchecibels, so you know when it's appropriate to bust out a can of STFU.

30 dB – Two dudes at the movie theater, whispering about banging the girl a few seats down.

50 dB – A single man screaming "Take it off!" during a spelling bee.

60 dB – Someone requesting "Freebird!" at the opera.

85 dB – A single man screaming "Yeehaw!" while riding a mechanical bull.

90 dB – A guy screaming "Let's do shots!" Let's douche *what?*

95 dB – A table of four at a loud restaurant, chanting "Eat it! Eat it!" at the poor bastard who's fighting the urge to regurge during a wing-eating contest.

100 dB – A bunch of tone-deaf dudes singing "Livin' on a Prayer" in a karaoke room.

120 dB – A 'roid head at the gym, screaming his way through a mild seizure.

135 dB – A crowd of twelve frat brothers barking drill instructions at a naked, dung-covered freshman during a hazing ritual (not including freshman's weeping).

140 dB – See above (including freshman's weeping).

145 dB – Arsenio Hall's "dogpound" in full "Woof" mode.

BINGIN' GENERAL'S WARNING

Anything in the zone of 1–100 douchecibels is harmless. Sure, it's annoying to have to hear the dudes at the table next to you blabber about the twins they scored while you try to romance your date, but who can blame them—the next best thing to bagging a girl is engaging in **baggadocio**.

Anything above 95 douchecibels may result in permanent hearing loss—shut that shit down immediately. But careful how you do it. Don't tell them to "bag it"—they're *already* bagging it: **douchebagging** it. As a rule, politely telling a douche to be quiet will only make him louder.

Douche: [Amusing his friends with a loud *Scarface* impression at a quiet restaurant] Is this it? Eating, drinking, fucking, sucking?

You: Dude, can you quiet down a little here? We're trying to eat our dinner.

Douche: [raising his voice 10 douchecibels]: What are you looking at? You're all a bunch of fucking assholes.

You: Dude, yeah, I've seen *Scarface*. Funny impresh. Could you just maybe keep it a little quieter?

Douche: [raising voice another 20 douchecibels] YOU NEED PEOPLE LIKE ME!

You: Okay, yeah . . . just . . .

Douche: YOU NEED A FUCKING ARMY IF YOU GONNA TAKE ME!

By this time his friends are hooting and hollering and the douchecibels have risen to a deafening, insurmountable roar.

Instead of trying to reason, try using French: *"Fermez la douche!"*

Douche: [doing his impression of *Lionheart* at a quiet restaurant] LIOOOOONHEEEEEART!!!!!!!!

You: Dude! *Fermez la douche!*

Douche: [Humbled, chastened. Doesn't quote another line from *Lionheart*.]

douchebrag – To brag about something douchey you've done, or to brag in a douchey manner. ("Dude, we've heard *five times* now about how you got a hummer in your Hummer. Stop douchebragging.") Also known as baggadocio.

douchebumps – When the hairs on the back of your neck stand up because of how douchey someone is: "That chode in the visor and the spiked hair gives me douchebumps."

douchecifer – An evil douche.

doucheflag – To flag someone's douchey behavior.

Before you **douchetag** someone, you should give them a chance to prove they're not actually a raving chodemeister. You might be tempted to think someone a douche when they tell you they like a certain Nickelback song, but come on—everyone has the occasional lapse in judgment (consider the fact that you bought this book). Simply flag the offense and go on "chotch watch." Then douchetag them if they do something douchetacular like get a "Nickelsack"—a **sacktoo** of the lead singer's face on their scrote.

exhibit gAy – Evidence that a dude is gay: "You like Cindy Lauper? Ladies and gentlemen of the jury, I present exhibit gAy. Not that there's anything wrong with that . . ."

guarantedious – Sure to be boring: "I have to go to my wife's sister's wedding reception. It's guarantedious."

guidon't – 1. A Guido-related faux-pas. 2. A command given to a Guido that he cease his Guido-related behavior.

Guidos are the bane of any night out. They're like roaches—once you see one **guitard** in a fitted, striped Club Monaco shirt and so much lube in his hair that he deserves a Nobel Grease Prize, there's sure to be more. You have to flee the Gui even if it means leaving behind your fourteen-dollar drink. That's why it's croosh to avoid clubs that have **guidoormen**—doormen who won't hesitate to let in a Guido, and will in fact bump chests with them as they lift the velvet rope. Of course, it's a doorman's very job to bar Guidos from entry so that the stylish and sexy can party in peace, but just like drug kingpins planting operatives inside of the PD, Guidos sometimes install one of their own inside of the club. Sometimes, instead of a DJ, the club has a *GuiJ* who spins cheesy techno music like "Castles in the Sky" (DJ Propecia Remix) and "Better Off Alone" (DJ Viagara Remix).

To help you know when you should tell a person "Guidon't," here's a list of some other **guidiculous** bullshit.

1. **Vagina shirts.** Guidon't wear button-down shirts with diagonal stripes forming a V (for Vagina) at the buttons.
2. **Crotch curtains.** Guidon't wear untucked button-down shirts that hang over the crotch.
3. **Jersey jerseys.** Guidon't wear any outfit that screams, "I'm from New Jersey."
4. **Hairticulture.** Excessive hair gel is a classic guidon't.
5. **Bluster clusters.** Guidon't bump chests with other dudes as if cruising for a contusing.
6. **Brocaine.** Guidon't snort bumps off of your fake Ferrari key and spend the next hours telling your bromos how much you love them.
7. **Brolling deep.** Unless it's a bachelor party, guidon't travel with ten other dudes.
8. **Man-tanorexia.** Guidon't spend too much time in the tanning booth, and turn your nads into orange Nerf balls.
9. **Guiodorant.** Guidon't be a cologne-ial oppressor by douching yourself in Axe body spray.
10. **Red Bull yell.** Guidon't stand around pounding Red Bull and yelling, "Yeeeah dude!" Red Bull gives you wings—because it transforms you into a giant fairy.
11. **Pecsibitionism.** Guidon't show off your pecs by wearing fitted shirts.
12. **Gianni Verchotchy.** Guidon't wear Italian designers like Diesel or Versace.

jesticles – Balls that are a joke.

lamedropper – Someone who pathetically tries to impress people by dropping names and such that are totally lame.

Ever wish a douche bell could go off every time some dude is conversing with you and he lamedrops? And it's not just names—maybe you're chilling in the break room, minding your own business, when the Dick from accounting walks in and tells you you look like shit. "You know what you need is a little R&R," he says. "I just got back from St. Barts (*ding ding ding! douche douche douche!*). Best five days of my life. Totally recommend it." Thanks for the advice, asshat, or were you just **bagvertising**—showing everyone what an insufferable douchebag you are?

Watch out for these common types of lamedrops:

1. **The A-bomb.** Drops the name of an A-lister, sometimes by first name.
2. **The business card drop.** Mentions someone's job title in order to impress you. "My friend John is head of Smegma, Inc. . . ."
3. **The food drop.** Mentions culinary terms like "flambé" and "tartar."
4. **The quaff drop.** Checks the microwbrew or fancy wine he's drinking.
5. **The stock market drop.** Mentions the stocks he has money in to show he's a high roller.
6. **The ball drop.** Goes out of his way to mention sports names and stats (usually to other guys) to show he's a superfan.
7. **The clothing drop.** Makes sure you're aware that he's wearing Prada or Armani.
8. **The tear drop.** Tells her that he cried during a certain book or movie. "When they tossed that guy's salad in *Deliverance*, I just . . . I couldn't help myself . . . a grown man crying . . ."
9. **The bad-habit drop.** "You're right, this is a good Bordeaux. But if you *really* want to get fucked up, I know a guy who has great black-tar heroin. Have you ever screwed a gimp hooker on that stuff?"
10. **The price drop.** "Sure valet parking is expensive, but when you own a $90,000 car, you want to take care of it . . ."
11. **The line drop.** The impressive line from a book or movie. "Was it Prince Bolkonski who said in *War and Peace*, 'Love hinders death. Love is life'? I think that's so true."
12. **The stop, drop, and roll.** In order to show you how awesome

he is, he stops the conversation, tells you he has to do or meet something or someone more important than you, and rolls.

motherchode – A dude who is the motherlode of chodedom.

nadmouth – 1. To stick your nads in someone's mouth, as in "Keep badmouthing me and I'll totally nadmouth you." 2. A mouth that reeks of someone's nads ("He's got the worst nadmouth I've ever smelled").

out to munch – Out to lunch, in the sense of being too busy munching butts to pay attention to the task at hand.

pleadiculous – So ridiculous it makes you go, "Bro, please."

pairoids – Something that causes you to grow a pair. ("Dude, what's up with the jesticles? Do I need to inject you with pairoids?")

PhDouche – Someone who has achieved the highest degree of douchieness.

power tool – The total tool who has achieved power, wealth, or fame.

Most tools start off strong by impressing potential employers with their toothy grins and firm **manshakes**, but once they've settled into the job it becomes obvious they're total Bluetools. That glowing roach in their ear is the only thing that separates them from the unwashed asses. They hang out at the bottom of the corporate ladder, happy to look up the skirts of everyone who rises above them. Eventually a merger or acquisition leaves them on the streets, where they continue to "reach out to the client" and asking him to "circle back"—even if all that means is asking strangers for change so they can buy just one more venti crapuccino.

Don't worry! If you're a total tool, there *are* ways to make your toolishness work for you until you become successful beyond your wildest wet dreams.

STRATEGY	TIME TILL YOU'RE A POWER TOOL	PROS	CONS	NOTABLE POWER TOOL
Business school	5–6 years	Increase your toolishness by learning buzzwords like "synergy"	Two years of cock shock, since 70% of MBA candidates are dudes	The Donald
Law school	6–7 years	Offer pro bono services to chicks and they'll sometimes perform "pro boner" work	Crippling debt may keep you from buying the **wanker tanker** of your dreams	Clarence Thomas
Socialite D.J.	1–3 Hamptons parties	Perpetually surrounded by drunk-ass rich bitches	Perpetually surrounded by drunk-ass rich bitches	D.J. A.M.
Rock star	5–6 guitar lessons	Sex, drugs	STDs; ODs	Ted Nugent
Politician	8–10 years	Showing interns your "filibuster"	Getting vetoed by said interns	George W. Bushmuncher

reprodouche – 1. To reproduce or mimick someone's douchey behavior, as if you're their **doppeldouche**. "Look at those two guys in the sombreros—did the first one reprodouche?" 2. To sire a child who will surely be as douchey as its father: "Dude, you're free to do whatever. Just promise me you won't reprodouche."

scattitude – A shitty attitude.

sketch artist – A guy or girl who is a master at being sketchy; they never get caught despite being shadier than a jacaranda tree.

snorgy – Something so boring it induces a veritable **snorchestra** of snoring: "My original philosophy professor really put the T&A in TA, but after she got fired for hooking up with me they replaced her with this total blowhard—and I don't mean 'blow hard' in the fun way. Now the class is a hardcore, three-hour snorgy."

stooper scooper – An opportunist who scoops up those who are temporarily stooping to his or her level. ("Bill only scored that chick because her ex dumped her and she wanted **v-venge**. He's a total stooper scooper.")

swignoramous – A drunken idiot.

tard evidence – Hard evidence that someone is a tard.

Tool Aid – What you drink in order to become a tool: "Dude, why are you friends with that douche?" "Bill used to be cool but then he went to business school and he really drank the Tool Aid."

tool bus – A stretch limo rented by a bunch of tools looking to tool around on a Saturday night. See also "wanker tanker."

totarded – Totally retarded (or **betarded**—beyond retarded).

Trek check – A way of telling your bro to STFU about *Star Trek* because you're not a sixteen-year-old dork anymore: "This is like that episode of *Star Trek* when . . ." "Dude! Trek check!" Note that this doesn't apply to *Star Wars*, which is *much* cooler.

tugly – So ugly you would rather go home and tug it to porn than do it with her.

Sure we've all heard the term "fugly," but it's about time we find some alternatives. Try these on for size.

- **Atrugly:** Atrociously ugly.
- **Bugly:** So ugly you feel like you're bugging out. She looks like something out of the bar scene in *Fear and Loathing in Las Vegas.*
- **Chugly:** So ugly you'd need to chug at least a pitcher to be able to do it with her.
- **Drugly:** So ugly you'd have to be *really* high to do her.
- **Hugly:** So ugly you'd rather give her a platonic hug goodnight than go home with her.
- **Knugly:** So ugly she looks like she just ate a knuckle sandwich.
- **Lugly:** So ugly she looks like a big lug.
- **Mugly:** So ugly she has mugged you of all of your faculties.
- **Rugly:** So ugly her face looks like it's been stepped on like a rug.
- **Slugly:** So ugly it looks like she got slugged in the face, maybe even with a Louisville Slugger.
- **Smugly:** So ugly she probably had to be smuggled into the club.
- **Stugly:** So ugly you feel sorry that she got stuck with that face.
- **Strugly:** So ugly you're struggling not to vomit.
- **Trugly:** So ugly it looks like her face got hit by a truck.
- **Ughly:** So ugly you go, "Ugh."
- **Zerugly:** So ugly you'd give her a zero on a scale of 1–10.

understandicapped – Totally dense.

vagigantic – As large as a very large vagina. This classier alternative to "ginormous" is used only for things that are immeasurably huge—the national debt, for instance—and best used to spice up a tired put-down: "You, my friend, are a vagigantic douche."

11

STYLINGUISTICS

(n.) Language that pertains to the elements of style

Who cares whether it's the clothes that make the man or it's the man that makes the clothes—what matters is that the clothes make a woman want to blow you. Style is what distinguishes us from apes, which is why it's counterproductive to wear a monkey suit. Instead, you should "get your sexy on" like Justin Timberlake says, "get your game on" like Trace Adkins says, "get your grown-man on" like Lil Wayne says—or at the very least put a goddamn shirt on so we don't have to look at those man cans.

The great thing about suiting up is that even the most clueless bastard can walk into Calvin Klein and buy a "wet suit"—a three-piece that really turns a woman on. And you don't even have to go that far. Jay-Z famously eschewed jerseys for a crisp pair of jeans and button-ups. And Tom Cruise demonstrated in *Cocktail* that even a Hawaiian shirt can be ginamite.

Still, a lot of dudes find it hard to assemble a scoredrobe or deal with even the most basic matters of guygiene—hence the "How to Get the Perfect Shave" article you see in men's mags every few months. What's next, "How to Wipe Your Ass When You're Out of Toilet Paper"? [If anyone at *GQ* is reading this, *call me*.] Case in point: Tons of **lidiots** think that baseball hats are the only thing you need to get a chick—it's fine to wear a lid to show allegiance for a favorite team, but when you start getting permanent hat head, think about how often you wear the thing and put a cap on it.

To do the do's and avoid the don'ts, you'll need to know what to call them. So let's take a look at the style guide.

ambiflexterous – Able to impress a girl by flexing multiple parts of the body.

bathlete – A man who goes to excessive lengths to bathe and groom himself, sometimes seen in **shornography**—pornos featuring **depubescent** dudes.

brawndescension – The condescension a brawny individual shows towards a less well-developed specimen: "My trainer said I was developing a nice three-pack, but I think he was being brawndescending."

cloutfit – An outfit that shows how much clout you have via French cuffs with twenty-four-karat links, a diamond-encrusted Brolex watch, a bespoke suit, polished wingtips, etc.

credlocks – Dreadlocks sported by a white dude to try to establish cred in the black community.

darecut – A haircut you get on a dare: "Dude! There's a penis shaved into your head!" "Yeah, it was a darecut. I get to use Tim's Lotus for a night if I go into work wearing this."

dickini – A male thong or Speedos that excessively reveal your **hairea**.

doucheshave – A shave befitting a douchebag.

flaircut – A haircut with flair.

flake rake – A comb when raked over the scalp of a **druffian**, or someone with lots of dandruff.

freeodorant – Emergency deodorant that you get for free by walking into the drug store and spraying or rubbing it on while no one is looking.

freetergent – Detergent you poach from other people in the laundromat because you're too broke to pay for a fifty-cent box of Tide.

fro pas – An afro that is a faux pas because it's worn by a total honky. Sometimes described as **frotesque**.

gut cheeks – When your gut is so big that when you sandwich it with both hands and push them together, a giant asscrack-like crease develops down the middle.

heteroflexual – A dude who spends as much time at the gym as a gay guy, but claims to be straight.

khakistani – One who religiously wears khaki. Khakistan refers to a place where khakistanis gather (for instance, Dockers commercials). "Whoa, when did we cross into Khakistan? We just turned onto pleats street in button-down town!"

It's important to make sure your wardrobe isn't a preppy boredrobe. There's nothing wrong with these labels, but wear them day in and day out and you'll become a Club Monabro, or a Banana Republican, or an Arbercrombie Zombie, or a Tommy Hilfrigger. Don't J. Crewcify yourself—wear nothing but J. Crew and you'll end up dating a **bag hag**.

It's not like you have to go *Queer Eye* or become a **retrosexual**— a dude who wears 1960s Savile Row suits and vintage silk handkerchiefs. Just make sure you don't become, for instance, a **Jeep creep**—a dude who constantly wears cargo shorts, mandals, a Polo shirt, and a backwards baseball hat like he's tooling around in a Jeep Wrangler circa 1989. And don't be a **tucknut**—a dorkass who tucks his shirt in even if he's in the pit at a Four Whorehounds of the Apocalypse concert. Especially egregious is the tit tuck, when you tuck your pants up high in order to use your belt as a makeshift girdle. If your moobs are getting belt burn, it might be time to hit the gym instead of blobfuscating.

kickhead – A sneaker freak who gets pumped every time he scores a new pair of vintage Reeboks.

You have to be pretty clueless to go around shoeless. Still, a lot of guys shoot themselves in the foot by wearing **slip-slops** (flip-flops can cause you to slip in the slop that's on the men's room floor). And they wonder why women shoo them away.

On the other end of the spectrum is the guy who tries to maintain "feet cred" by collecting every limited-edition Nike ever made. He's a real "swoosh douche." It's good to put your best foot forward by rocking a pair of "pick-up kicks"—sick kicks that make women drop to your feet and worship the ground you walk on. You can even buy two pairs of them to avoid "dunk funk," the "sneak reek" that occurs when you wear the same hightops every day. Just make sure you don't start hordin' Jordans like you're the Imelda Marcos of basketball shoes.

lidiot – An idiot obsessed with collecting baseball caps.

mandicap – A handicap that a man has to overcome in order to get with a girl.

Any flunkey can score a girl by hitting the gym, throwing on a striped button-down, and splashing on some Old Spice that reminds her of Daddy. What really makes you a man is if you can roll around in ape shit, barf on yourself from the horrible stench of it, eat some of the shit to get the puke taste out of your mouth, gargle with ass juice, and *still* get a girl to go downtown. This is why firemen are the height of masculinity—they get chicks despite the lingering odor of charred cat flesh.

What are some typical mandicaps? First of all—**blunderwear**, underwear that kill any chances you might have. Tighty whities are a classic example, but even worse is **tighty shities**. Hide those sickening chundergarments! As soon as you know your pants are going to come off, excuse yourself to the bathroom, stash the skivvies somewhere, and return to the **mise-en-obscene** in freeball mode. Ideally you'll be able to hide them somewhere where they'll be clean the next day. Just remember to retrieve them before she does, or you might wake up to a chick asking you, "Why are there SpongeBob SquarePants boxers in my dishwasher?"

Another typical mandicap is the beer gut. You can only suck it in so much—at a certain point you're going to have to explain it away. Tell her that you're bloated because earlier in the day you participated in a hot-dog-eating contest for charity. The focus will quickly shift from your grotesquely distended navel to your compassion for kids with Tucker-Chan Disease.

Women are also turned off if you're **pubiquitous**—meaning your short and curlies are all over the place. It's fine to have a Hairway to Heaven running from your gut to your nuts, but as far as the nuts themselves, why not clip before you strip? You also might want to shave that **hairriere**. Remember, everyone is wary of going anywhere near a **hairorrist**—a mofo whose terrifying amount of hair makes him look like he's been hiding in an Afghan cave for six months.

Even more deadly in this area is bad guygiene. There's a thin line between smelling manly and being so **choderiferous** that you reek of unwashed chode. A girl who's kissing you from your neck to your pecs to your pecker might just stop dead in her tracks when she catches a whiff of your "smelly button." And don't be surprised when even the most enthusiastic "odor eater"— a girl who will go down on you no matter how much your dink stinks— draws the line at your "foul balls." Not all girls are into getting "garbage bagged." Luckily there's a product that will prevent your pocket rocket from becoming a stink bomb: Irish Spring deodorant. It can be quickly applied to the "bone zone" in the hairiest of situations and since it smells like soap, girls will never suspect you've tainted your taint with harmful chemicals.

Of course it goes without saying that the amount of time you spend combing yourself depends on how comely she is. If she's a perfect ten, spend at least ten minutes grooming. If she's a five, spend five. And if she's a one, it's fine to simply "douche your bag" by quickly washing your scrote in her sink, so long as you don't leave behind any stray pubes that might cause her to wonder whether you pounded it to her rubber ducky.

manties – "Man panties" you're forced to use when clean underwear aren't available after a hook-up and going commando is not an option.

There's no shame in slipping your dong into a thong when you're suffering from a bad bangover. Men have been wearing the pelts of the animals they've conquered since the dawn of dudes, and getting her Hanes on you is the ultimate screwvenir. But before you put your wood into her Frederick's of Hollywood, weigh your options:

ADVANTAGES OF MANTIES:

1. **Much cheaper than having to buy new undies.**
2. **Increased self-confidence.** When your boss tells you you've messed something up, you can think to yourself, "Whatever,

Viagravator. I'm wearing manties right now because I bagged your assistant last night."

DISADVANTAGES OF MANTIES:

1. **VML (Visible Manty Line).**
2. **Lack of breathing space may result in unsightly wedgies or "junk funk."**
3. **Unhappy realization that your package is small enough to fit into women's underwear, or that the girl you bagged has a bigger waist size than you.** Your cock stock may also plummet in her eyes: It may confirm her suspicion that you have a **weenis**.
4. **In the case of girls you never want to see again, it is not proper form to keep manties she thinks you're going to give back.** It is fine to mail them back to her, but only when they're accompanied by a nice note.
5. **It's easy to forget you're wearing manties, which can lead to mortal shame when you drop trou at the urinal.** Your coworkers may end up thinking you're a Marv—a disciple of famed basketball play-by-play man and renowned panty-wearing ass-biter Marv Albert.
6. **Girl may eventually turn on you and release trimtelligence to your bromos that you like to wear panties.** Bromos might not believe you when you insist they were *man*ties.
7. **If you end up hooking up with another girl that day, she's going to wonder why you're wearing another chick's panties.** Remember to pocket them before you take your pants off, and don't forget they're in your pocket the next day, or you may have a bad scene while you're fishing for change.

meodorant – Your own odor, worn in lieu of deodorant—often a form of **fleeodorant**, in that it causes people to flee from you.

Morrison Hotel – A figurative place that you check into in order to let the beard grow, the gut go, and the booze flow—much like Jim Morrison during the time he made the album of the same name.

must-not-stache – An unbecoming mustache.

nadequate – Offering ample breathing room for your nads. When selecting pants, choose a pair with plenty of "sack slack," otherwise you might just end up nadvertising. And moose knuckle isn't your only concern—things could also get very choderiferous. If your ball sweat moistens the crotch of your pants and you lose that "nuts-so-fresh feeling," you could end up walking into a meeting smelling like "cloth broth." Over time you might even develop a **jeangina**—a vagina-like gash that opens up in the crotch of your jeans after you've worn them for way too long.

pec check – When you check to make sure your pecs are still there by flexing first the right and then the left one—usually a move to impress girls.

pecscessive – Excessive as pertains to pecs or other muscles— overly developed: "Dude, it's one thing to be gympressive, but another thing to be totally pecscessive. You're going to scare girls away with those 'jock paps'!"

pecspert – An expert in matters of pecs and other muscles, e.g. a personal trainer: "Dude, if I keep gaining weight in my man cans I may need to call on your pecspertise."

plug ugly – Ugly due to fake hair.

sandwich board – Someone who wears team signage on both their front and back via a t-shirt and a backwards baseball hat.

scareline – A hairline that's receding so quickly it scares you every time you look at it. Considered a **stareline** when it's receding so quickly you feel like people are staring at it.

shampoop – Shitty shampoo.

stache gash – A gash of skin in your mustache, usually the result of shaving drunk or hungover.

starmoire – An armoire full of clothes that make you look like a rock star: "I got a date tonight with this girl who's totally out of my league. I'm really going to have to dig into the starmoire."

strip flop – When you strip off a tight shirt and your belly flops out—a sign that it's time to lose some weight.

tanachronism – A person, usually a chick but sometimes a dude like George Hamilton, who looks so tan they seem to be from another time (i.e. summer instead of winter).

12

TECHSPRESSIONS

(n.) Expressions that pertain to technology

It's a little known fact that Alexander Graham Bell invented the telephone while drunk off his ass. After killing a bottle of Mad Dog and chasing it with a shot of battery acid one night, he puked all over his crotch and made the first call in history to his assistant Thomas Watson to say, "Dude, come here! You gotta see this!" Bell later cleaned up the story, claiming he accidentally spilled the battery acid on his pants before calling his bro, but either way that first convo established the telephone as a powerful means of brommunication—a tradition that carried on into the age of the Batphone and was most memorably demonstrated by those dudes in the Bud commercial who said, "Whasssssuuuuup."

Of course, these days telephones are used pretty much exclusively by light-skinned black chicks, as Maddox rightly pointed out in his essay "Nine Things I Learned about the World according to Anonymous Stock Photo Models." There are only a few remaining means of **fellacommunication**: Ham radios, CB radios, those squad radios that marines carry around when they're laying waste to foreign lands, and the two-way radios that pilots use to tell their control center how friggin stoned they are. Oh yeah, there's also the "red phone" in the Oval Office.

But just because you aren't Commander in Chief doesn't mean you can't use technology to communicate in a manly manner. Texting, instant messaging, and e-mailing are other ways to demonstrate your prowess.

AIMbarassment – Embarrassment resulting from the misuse of AOL Instant Messenger.

When a girl you're avoiding e-mails to ask you out, you have about an hour to formulate a fake excuse as to why you can't. When she IMs you, however, that window of time is reduced to about twenty seconds. This is why you should never give a girl your AIM handle.

Another reason is this: Let's say you want to tell Barbara074 that you can't wait to run your hands through her blonde hair, but you accidentally send the message to Betty078, the brunette you're dating. You realize your mistake and say, "Um, didn't you mention something about dyeing your hair?" Not even that is going to save you from an **IMbroglio**. These "instant messes" are twice as likely to happen when you're **AIMing high**, so avoid online bongversations.

IMs are even more deadly if your girl has **Maccess**—access to your Mac. If you leave your IM running while she's using your pute pute, there's a good chance she'll **IMpersonate** you, pretending to be you when a buddy IMs. Take this conversation, in which your girlfriend is an **IMposter** posing as you, Studguy50:

Sexysadie: Hey babEdoll.
Studguy50: Hello?
Sexysadie: So can U get that sweater back from your girlfriend somehow? I know you told her U bought it for her after she found it in your bedroom but it's one of my favorites.

Studguy50: ??

Sexysadie: Or at least pay me 4 it? Maybe you can snag some $$ from her purse like that time you paid for my Brazilian?

Studguy50: ??????

Sexysadie: Um, R U OK sweetpea?

**Studguy50 has signed off. And is about to get his balls ripped off.

When you're IMing friends and your girl is in the room, be careful that she doesn't participate in **messagepianoge**. If she *does* peep over your shoulder while you're typing, make sure to **window wipe**:

Studguy50: /
Studguy50: \
Studguy50: /
Studguy50: \
Studguy50: /
Studguy50: \
Studguy50: /
Studguy50: \

Et voilà—the text is cleared from the IM window and your **IMterlocutor** knows that your girlfriend is in the room.

baller ID – An expression used to indicate that the person who is calling is a true baller: "How'd you know it was me?" "I saw you on baller ID, player."

bonecall – A booty call: "Man, this party is at maximum cockupancy, let me make a quick bonecall."

dickspatch – An email sent to your bros bragging about a bagging. Dickspatches are informative documents that allow your bros to live vagicariously through you and realize how awesome you are. They should be sent only on a "need-to-bro" basis, and not to recipients who'll violate brotocol by forwarding them to interlopers. Not only can this get your balls boiled by your girl, but it could end up all over the net or worse still as Exhibit A in divorce court. If you often send out dickspatches, create an anonymous e-mail address with a generic name like Mister Fister. Don't mention last names, company names, school affiliations, MySpace handles, or anything else super-specific in the text of the dickspatch. If you have to use your work email, make sure to use obscure Britishisms like "minge" in lieu of words that will easily clue in the spies in IT. Also, sexaggeration is always fine, but keep them halfway believeable or your bros will suspect your telling "tail tales."

Flutie text – A booty text that has about the same chances of ending in a score as Doug Flutie's Hail Mary pass did.

inboxquisition – An investigation into your inbox that ends in her putting the screws to you after she finds out you screwed someone else.

LapQuest – When you MapQuest directions to a strip club because it's in a shady, unfamiliar part of town.

liePhone (aka guyPhone) – A phone used for purposes of lying.

If lying is a crime, one's cell phone is very often the weapon of choice. As with any weapon, you just need to keep it from blowing up—and not "blowing up" as in getting a lot of booty calls. No, exploding in your face and ruining your life. Which often happens after you get a lot of booty calls.

Apparently Steve Jobs doesn't get many blow jobs, because his impressive little iPhone spends more time cockblocking than call blocking. The first problem is that everyone wants to play with this shiny toy and once it's in Curious Kathy's little hands, there's no way to keep her from seeing your booty texts, your latest e-mail from AdultFriendFinder, and of course your blowtographs (photographs of you getting blown).

Whether you own an iPhone or a **MackBerry**, observe the following rules to insure that a phone call isn't your downfall.

1. **Keep it in your pants.** Don't put your phone on the dinner table like someone in a Western does with his gun. Or be prepared to explain it to your girlfriend when a text message pops up saying, "Cum over & cum all over me? teehee."

2. **Never leave a phone behind.** When you deuceappear, don't leave your liePhone charging, or next thing you know it'll be your girlfriend charging straight at you with a knife. When you leave your phone unattended, it sends out an imaginary text message to your girl's brain, triggering a conversation which ironically enough resembles a booty text of sorts:

Your phone: CUM OVER – NEED U BAD.
Your girl: HAHA. REALLY?? DON'T KNO IF I SHLD.
Your phone: TOTES. HURRY CUM OVER.
Your girl: BRIAN WILL GET MAD : (
Your phone: ITS FINE. HE DUSN'T HAVE 2 NO.
Your girl: HMMM. OK. :)
Your phone: BRING YR READING GLASSES. ;)

If you come out of the bathroom and your girl is glaring at you, you can bet it's not just because of the tank stank.

3. **Put it on "liebrate."** Vibrators are a *man*'s best friend, too. After you feel the "good vibrations" of a booty call in your pants, give the girl you're with a few minutes to wrap up her vagibberish and then excuse yourself to the bathroom (your command center) to discretely check out the "ball call" you've received.

4. **Send and deceive.** Running to and from the bathroom every time you get a text is going to make her suspicious—and you may end up blowing a lot of money tipping the restroom attendant. When you have no choice but to text at the table,

use a palibi: "Sorry, my brother is asking me for our mom's gumbo recipe. He's trying to impress this girl he really likes." She'll find it cute, meaning you can text throughout the entire meal. You: "So sorry, now he's asking what prawns are. He's so retarded about cooking—he doesn't understand you can just substitute shrimp." Her: "Aww, you guys are so sweet." Your text: "Definitely want 2 bang U. Talk after dinner."

5. **Bad reception = Bad deception.** When you fail to take a girl's calls because some other girl is taking your balls, you're going to be tempted to lie that your phone was off, or your battery died, or you didn't have reception. You can pretend you were **talkupied** with someone on the other line but girls know the inner workings of your phone better than the person who had to repair it that last time it fell in the toilet while you were pulling a "puke-and-dook." They know exactly how many times it does or doesn't ring when it's on or off, and they know exactly how to tell if you've put them "under your thumb" by pressing "ignore." If a girl puts you on **hojak** by calling you over and over again until you pick up, your only option is to find the nearest railroad tracks, wait for the next train to come, throw it under the wheels, and present the shards to her the next day as proof that you had no way of picking it up.

6. **Be discrete—delete, delete, delete.** Guys often save filthy messages because they want to keep them as **do-venirs,** or so they can accurately quote their booty texts in the next day's dickspatch. Problem is, these words can and will come back to haunt you when your girl goes into your call log while you're dropping a log. And it's doubtful she'll buy your defense of "bent went sent."

obliterature – Literature composed while completely obliterated, usually on a cell phone.

There comes a point in every person's evening when he develops a **ginflated** sense of his writing ability and fancies himself a "man of letters," albeit letters that are very rarely in the right order. He becomes a regular F. Shots Fitzgerald and immediately self-publishes his drunken wisdom via e-mail or text. Here, for instance, is a typical outbox:

> 1:30 a.m. WASTED. 5 shots of tekeela is what eye TASTED.
> 1:45 a.m. Going home now. Going homo now!!!! Put ur cock in my eye sock.
> 1:50 a.m. Who let the dogs out? SERIOUSLY.
> 2:00 a.m. bout to skeet on the street, call a skeetsweeper. labyrinth of pennyloafers.
> 2:15 a.m. Dude, U R a men amung men.
> 2:30 a.m. Just vomited on hairless heiress, looks like baby rat
> 2:45 a.m. don't know where I am. eating green eggs + ham. Meet me in St. Louis.
> 3:00 a.m. If baloney is fake ham, what is phony baloney?
> 3:15 a.m. swimming in deep end of vomit pool.
> 4:00 a.m. Hello? If you know the person who owns this phone, he is passed out on the corner of 14th and Main. You might want to come fast, he has no pants on.

If you're a frequent author of **textcrement**, make sure your Outlook is set up to defer message delivery until at least an hour after you've hit send—that should give you plenty of time to sober up and squash that 2 a.m. message to your boss demanding a "raze or a promoshun."

PDA-hole – A total a-hole who is obsessed with his Personal Digital Assistant, to the point of BlackBerrying during conversations, while on the pot, or in the sack.

A lot of dudes think PDAs are ginamite when they're often nothing more than harbingers of douchebaggery, even if they no longer come with that PalmPilot "wand" that magically points out a-holes. In fact, when you use them in a dark place (a bar, a bedroom—anywhere you should be going down on a girl instead of sending texts) they literally light up your face like the search for Public Chotchmeister #1 has led to a foxhole and oh shit, there he is.

It's fine to text everyone you know that you're sitting next to Clay Aiken. It's when the BlackBerry leaves the buddy booth and enters the social sphere that it becomes a problem. Maybe you've worn a Bluetooth headset during intercourse. Or penned a break-up letter that ended with "sent from my BlackBerry wireless handheld." Maybe you've juiced your phone at a relative's funeral. Or sexted your back-up booty as soon as it became apparent that your Nerve date wasn't into DADV. Worse still, maybe you've used your Treo as a glowstick at a nightclub. If any of these is the case, you're a PDA-hole: Take one of those wildly twiddling thumbs and stick it where the ClearTouch Anti Glare™ screen don't shine.

On the chart of evolution, we can now add a devolved species next to upright man: The upright man who is stooped over a BlackBerry. The good news is, nature has a way of weeding out PDA-holes. They walk into speeding cabs while cleaning out their in-boxes. Or their Sidekick address book gets posted on the internet.

sendthusiasm – A girl's boundless enthusiasm for sending you annoying e-mails.

Never give a girl your e-mail address at work: if she's the sort who sends you five hundred e-mails a day, she'll cause your in-box to get full and bounce messages from other girls you're seeing. It only gets worse when you practice **responsenility** and forget to respond to her she-mails. That's when she starts sending you e-mails saying "Did you get my e-mail?" "Did you get my e-mail to your personal e-mail asking if you got my e-mail to your work e-mail?" "Did you get my voice mail asking if you got my e-mail to your personal e-mail asking if you got my e-mail to your work e-mail?" and so on into infinity. You begin to wonder how she can hold down a job while sending you a thousand e-mails a day—unless of course she works at Naggers Inc. in which case she is probably due for a promotion to Associate Vice President of Crawling Up Your Ass.

smell phone – A cell phone that has been stuffed down another man's pants and has taken on the odor of "junk funk," for instance a PDA that has been rubbed on the scrote to become a **SackBerry**. Stuffing another man's stuff down your pants—especially those that may end up in or near his mouth—is a quick and easy way to establish dominance by giving him your case of Hepatitis A. It's also a pretty amusing **sacktical joke**. In addition to cell phones, writing utensils can be stuck up the bunghole ("No. 2 pencils") or rubbed on the crotch ("Dick Bics").

spamouflage – Camouflage that causes you to click on spam mail by promising you naked photos, etc.

textermination – Terminating your relations with a chick via text message.

When you cut things off with a girl via SMS you can pretty much make up whatever excuse you want, phrase it in the most convincing manner, and there's no chance you'll experience the age-old "hump or dump" dilemma that occurs when you intend to break things off with a girl but she shows up to the restaurant wearing her "break-up makeup" and her hottest ho couture

When texterminating a girl, make sure your break-up messages don't go over fifteen words, or certain phones will break them up into two text messages and you'll be charged an extra five cents.

Standard texterminations:

Luv U but not IN luv w U
I thot I wuz red-E to date again but after my last gf Im not

sur I can trust any1 enuff 2 B in a rel8ionship. That kool?
I lyk u a lot but u r not wut im looking 4.
Lez B frends? ;)
Sorry but I found sum1 Ls
Do U hav ur frend Jens #?

textrovert – One who is extroverted when it comes to texting people.

A lot of folks believe texting is for teenage girls and grown men have no business doing it because it requires small fingers—and you know what they say about small fingers. Texting with your bro is especially awkward when you set off his pocket vibe. However communicating via **SMS-peranto**, the universal language of SMS messaging, can be a **texthilirating** way to show off your impeccable charm and dashing wit when it comes to dick jokes.

Once you've acquired a fair amount of **textpertise**, you'll find it's quite easy to **textpedite** basic things like making plans to go to the club with your bros. They can respond to your texts immediately, rather than having to wait for their girl to leave the room so they can call. Sure, often your bros are slow to respond, which can be a **textcrutiating** in light of your high **texpectations**, but if you **textcoriate** them they'll get quicker and soon enough your cell will be **textploding**—blowing up with text messages.

Here's an example of a typical **textchange** between bros:

Bro #1: Strip club at 1:00? Happy hour!
Bro #2: jg#I$UTJjggklaaaa
Bro #1: Wha?
Bro #2: Sorry, textcrement.
Bro #1: Ah okay.
Bro #2: Yes, strip club at 1. PS check this new **textpression**.
Bro #1: ??
Bro #2: ====8 ~o ~o ~o :>0
Bro #1: Haha TXTCELLENT!

When texting, be aware that certain abreevs are SFC (Strictly For Chicks). Use "obvi" or "whatevs" and you're basically saying "Obvi I have no balls whatsoevs." Same goes with LOL ("I'm Laughing Out Loud because where my balls should be there is just a windy cavern"), OMG ("Oh My God, my balls have suddenly disappeared") and ROFL ("Rolling On Floor Looking for my balls.") It's highly Q (questionable) to use any of these in a convo—you are spitting in the face of every soldier who ever got his limbs blown off without saying, "OMG!"

Some abreevs can and *should* be busted out, as the following sentence shows:

"No presh, but this drinking sesh is a croosh ocaij—it'd be an unfortch sitch if you pussed. Don't be a DB. Preesh!"

If your bro does end up pussing out, respond with: "Traj" (tragic) or "vaj" (you are a vagina).

Of course, rules against using chick expreshes can be bent when you're having an IM conversash with an actual chick. Feel free to use "xoxoxox" as long as it means "I'm going to bite (x) and suck (o) on your tits." And if you have to use idiotic emoticons, at least do it in a somewhat masculine manner by doling them out hierarchically, according to a star system.

SMILEY STARS

☺ – She tells you her STD test came back clean.
☺ ☺ – She tells you, Maury Povich–style, "You are not the father."
☺ ☺ ☺ – She tells you she and her "slutty friend Monica" are coming over, can you buy a nice Pinot Noir?
☺ ☺ ☺ ☺ - She tells you she and her slutty friend are bringing over some mescal.

Be careful to delete exchanges such as the above—once again, you're screwed if your girlfriend **textcavates** your in-box, **tex-**

trapolates some bullshit after reading suspicious messages, and accuses you of being up to no good.

One last word of advice—chicks love it when you "ciao down" by using the word "ciao." No girl can resist a ciao burger hot off the grill:

(| ciao |)

Especially when it's served with lettuce:

(|{ ciao }|)

Or maybe she'd prefer a ciaokabob?

-----c-i-a-o-

And always ask if she'd like a ciaotini to go with that:

0---<| ciao

Or, on special occasions, some ciaopagne:

POP!! Ciao o o   o o o ooooo

Every girl loves a Doogie Ciaoser. So to paraphrase Snoop Dogg, "ciao till the next episode."

SACKNOWLEDGMENTS

Sacknowledgments (n.) An expresh of gratitude to everyone I know with a ball sack, and okay—some chicks, too.

I'd like to thank the fine folks who helped with this piece of obliterature, in no particular order except for penis size. First, a HELLS YEAH to Stirling Snow, my brollaborator since middle school. A heart-felt YOU DA MAN to Brett Valley, maker of publishing history. BIG UP YASELF to Brando Skyhorse, for putting aside his own brilliant book, *Flexicans* (a workout guide for Mexicans), to come up with *hot dog* and countless other words of wisdom. A heartfelt YOU'RE MONEY, BABY to my agent Jud Laghi for being unflappable. An earnest NICE ONE to the first editor who number-closed this book, Adam Korn, and the dude who got his sloppy seconds, Matthew Benjamin. They are righteous bros. An enthusiastic PREESH to everyone at Collins including Laura Dozier and to *the one*, Anne Cole, whose thoughtful, sympathetic editing of this book proves that chicks dig it. A big THANKS DUDE to Liza Monroy, who let me write part of it (on a roll of toilet paper) in Jack Kerouac's former home in Borelando, Florida. A big I LOVE YOU, BRO to Pablo Maurer, author of some of my favorite words—like *battleshipping* and *troll stroll*—as well as all of the truly vile and despicable ones. (Yes,

I'm making him my **scapescrote**.) My father and guydol Christopher Maurer offered helpful suggestions, none of which, surprisingly, were "Burn this before your mother reads it," and my mom Maria Estrella Iglesias, who is of course an exception to all of the ginaralisms in this book, is my answer to anyone who reads it and thinks, "He must not have been loved as a child." One of the dictionary definitions of a "neologism" is "a meaningless word coined by a psychotic," and without the support of my bros and those who broed along, I truly would've descended into insanity: A big YOU ROCK to Amina Akhtar, Aimee Bianca, Angelo "Jean Gina" Fabara, Ed "Benderdome" Mullins, Jessica Pilot, Amber Qureshi, Daniel "The Hulk" Ricciato, Kyona Watts, and Jason Wishnow. Lastly, a WHAT'S UP, 'DOCH to Rupert Murdoch. He wanted the title to be *Matecabulary*, but with all dude respect, I think mine is perior.